The last sultan

Marjet Maks

The last sultan
@Marjet Maks

Cover @Laura Holden 2023
Cover photo, bee-eater @Rashuli/CC-BY-2.0 2013
Layout text: @Marjet Maks 2023
Editing: Sherry Oxley and Maryke Hines

ISBN: 978-90-822119-7-9

The last sultan is self-published by Marjet Maks and was first published in Dutch in 2013 as *De zucht van de Moor*

'Just as the blossom is the precursor of the fruit, so one's youth is the promise of his life'

Reshad Feild, The Last Barrier

CONTENTS

LA ALPUJARRA

Lost

*I*n the valley, the evening light reflected red against the rocks worn by wind, sun, and rain. In their black shadows, I suspected deep caves that were not visible from where I stood. I fantasised how the Moors would have hidden from the Christians in those caves and how they would have left their treasures: gold and diamonds or even forbidden Islamic manuscripts that I would find.

Sam sat next to me and with a glance at the dashboard clock, she heaved a sigh. 'Are you all right?' I shifted back to second gear just before a sharp turn.

'Pff no, I'm carsick.'

'Sorry Squirrel, you want me to stop for a minute?' After the curve I kept driving slowly, hoping to see an indent on the narrow country road.

'Let's drive to La Parra; I'm longing for a shower and a glass of wine.'

'Don't you want to stretch your legs?'

'Later will be early enough, right?' She gave me a convincing smile.

'Hard to imagine, isn't it?'

'What?' Sam yawned.

'That the Moors used to walk around here in silk robes, and were reading, writing, knew about astronomy, you name it, while we - up in the north - were still deeply immersed in the Middle Ages.'

'Here we go again. Please, Jacob. It was a long day.'

'Not even five centuries ago, the Moors and Christians slaughtered each other in this lovely landscape.'

'Jacob, stop it! I don't give a damn about the past and those bloody war scenes you fantasise about. I want to enjoy. It's so beautiful here.'

'Just wait until we get to the Alhambra, and Spanish history will fascinate you too.' I gave her knee a friendly squeeze.

'Me? Never,' Sam said. 'Yes, I love the Spanish food, and yes, the sun and beautiful nature, but your attraction to history, never!'

'True. You're attracted by another idea.'

She gave me thé look. Rolling eyes, pursed lips.

'But with kids, we don't have this freedom, honey. We would be at a children's playground or a crowded swimming pool in some tourist center with our feet in a lukewarm wading pool, gawking at our cute toddler.'

'Brat. Why are you so nasty. I want kids, yes, and I want them with you.'

'Wrong idea, you know that, squirrel.'

'Enough!' Sam, annoyed, grabbed the door as if she wanted to get out.

I stepped on the brake, steered the Nissan Micra onto a dirt road, parked and turned off the engine. I got out, stretched my legs, and took in a deep breath of fresh air. The immensity of the mountain range Sierra Nevada rose up behind me. Two eagles circled above the valley. There was absolute silence, and suddenly, I realised I was insignificant: a grain of sand, a breeze of air. It was an overwhelming emotion, and I stood motionless for a moment.

I walked down the dusty trail; the sheer cliffs luring me in the glowing light, again I imagined that no one had been in those caves for the last five hundred years and that I would discover something special: a sacred stone or an ancient Quran.

Sam came behind me and yanked my arm: 'I don't want this, Jacob; Camilla is waiting for us at the Bed & Breakfast. We should have been in La Parra by now. We will be too late for dinner and I want my shower, remember?'

'Just a stroll. They never eat here before ten, we have lots of time. Camilla can wait, as far as I'm concerned.'

After the next corner, I turned right at a fork in the road, I took the left trail twice and walked further down, and right again. Or had it been left three times? The air conditioning in the car had blown cold air, I had no idea of the temperature outside. This was southern Spain in August; late afternoon and the sun still had the power of an air fryer. Sam always paid attention and had a better sense of direction than I did, but today she was absent-minded and followed me, sulking.

The sky became translucent, in another hour, it would be dark. I felt guilty and turned to my girlfriend. I'm sorry, Squirrel. We're lost. We have walked this path before, haven't we? I have no idea which way to go back.'

'Shit! You're so stupid. You're so damned stubborn. You have no sense of direction. Why did I follow you? In my flip flops, without a hat, without water. It is your fault. You never know where you are. You are a dreamer and drive absent-minded. You never cook, you wash the dishes, then return them half-dirty to the cupboards. You just do what you feel like!

'What the hell does that have to do with getting lost.'

'Nothing. I'm sick and tired of this life with you.' Seething, Sam turned right into a path that rose sharply and disappeared behind a rock.

'And you just told me you want my child.' I sighed. 'We certainly shouldn't go that way, Sam.' But I followed her anyway, with my tail between my legs. Of course, she was right. Sam was always right; the ancient olive trees along the path told me so too. Their twisted faces, carved into the capricious trunks, were yelling at me: 'Asshole!'

Further on, Sam sat whimpering on a stump. She'd sprained her ankle. More bad luck to tackle. But this path looked familiar to me. Hopeful, I walked past her and felt her murderous look burning into my back. 'Don't get lost,' she yelled after me. I'm not taking another step!'

Her eternal criticism. Me, the clumsy fool, she the feminist who took care of it all. Well, that's what she thought of herself. She wanted nothing more than to follow in her mother's footsteps and become the matriarch of a large family. At the beginning of our relationship, she found me endearing. Later, she hoped she could change me. Which, of course I didn't want to; I'm not stupid. Besides, I had a rather dominant mother, and Sam's traits felt suspiciously familiar.

Ever since we lived together, I've missed my freedom. Everything had to be her way, her rules, her routine. When she swept the floor, and I walked through her pile of dust, lost in thought, she shouted irritably: 'Watch out, dude. Didn't you learn anything from your mother?' No, because we didn't have a floor to sweep, at least not when I was around; besides, my mother had servants. Sam came from a large rural Irish family, Catholic, of course. Father, mother, sisters, brothers, it was always a happy mess where I felt like the neighbor who had come to visit at the wrong time.

'If you can laugh, make love and work together, your relationship will be successful.' That's what Inez, my mother, always said after I'd introduced my latest girlfriend to her. 'But don't forget to look at her mother, because at the end of the day, every girl will look like her mom.' Maybe she had said that one time too often. Sam had caught me in her nets. I liked her energy and fell for her green eyes with small brown flecks, like the freckles on her cheeks. I called her 'Squirrel' because of her auburn hair, which she mostly wore in a ponytail. Sam's cheerful nature drew me out of my gloomy moods. She knew what was good for me; better than I knew myself. Meanwhile, I thought she was starting to look more and more like her mother: a sturdy woman with eight children who reads the Ladies' Home Journal cover to cover. Sam didn't do that yet, but I expected her to be that way in a few years.

I got to the top of the hill and suddenly had a wide view. To the left and right of the path an open field interrupted the rows of olive trees. Heaps of stones and chunks of rock laying in the yellowed grass. Bees buzzed in lavender bushes, and above my head came a strange high-pitched sound.

Frirrt, frrirt. A group of birds with pointed wings swarmed over. Something yellow glittered in the low light. They were beautiful and flew around me as if they wanted to show me the way and tell me their story. Fascinated, I stood still, until something shifted in the corner of my eye: a dark shadow moved towards me. Immediately I was awake again.

A man. Thank God! That guy probably could take us back to the car.

'Hola,' I shouted cheerily.

'Buenas tardes.' The man approached quickly among the groves of thyme and lavender. He took their scent with him on his trouser legs. We had discovered that people in this Spanish hinterland did not speak a word of English, so I tried to formulate a sentence with the few words of Spanish I knew.

'Perdido, mujer over there, ankle.' I gestured behind me from where I had come from. '

Are you lost?' he asked.

I didn't know what I heard and stammered: 'You speak English?'

'Si, si. Have English woman.' Grinning cheerily, he showed me the black holes between his teeth that reminded me again of the caves I had wanted to discover. He was thin and shabbily dressed, and his greasy grey hair was tied in a ponytail. He seemed a few years older than me.

The man said: 'Come on, let's have a drink.'

I licked my dry lips and watched the sky turning inky blue above the steeply rising field. 'Wow, I don't know; my wife is over there, we need to move on.'

The man shrugged and walked with me down the path to Sam, who was still sitting exactly as before, but jumped up when she saw us coming.

'Ha, nice. Jacob, will he take us to the car?'

'Yes, very soon. He invited us for a drink.'

'Great, I'm thirsty as hell.' Sam limped on my arm. The man, unmistakably a gypsy, walked ahead, rattling on incessantly in a medley of Spanish and English. It didn't make much sense to me.

At the point where I'd met him, he paused until we were standing next to him, then he stepped among the rocks, clumps of grass, and bushes of wild herbs. It was only now that I saw a path winding through it. Sam walked ahead of me, following the man. The sharp twigs of the bushes scraped her bare legs, but she barely limped. A little adventure, and she didn't have time to worry about herself.

The Ruin

The evening breeze brushed my face and was almost cool and refreshing. At the top of the hill, was the same spacious view I had seen before. To the right, high above us, I saw our rental car against the background of the sky. Less than ten minutes' walk as the crow flies. To the left, there was the rough, sand-colored wall of a ruin. In a pool, water was shining in between high reed plumes, and I heard frogs croak.

The man stopped.

Sam tried her Spanish on him: 'Es muy romántico aquí.'

In reply, he whistled shrilly, and immediately a not-to-be neglected herd of fierce-looking dogs came running after him. They barked and wagged their tails as if their master had been gone for hours.

Sam wasn't a softie, I had once seen her slaughter a chicken on her parents' farm without shedding a tear, but she was terrified of dogs.

'Jacob, I'm not going any further,' she squeaked and slipped her hand into mine.

'It's okay. No pasa nada,' the man said. And indeed, he clicked his tongue, snapped his fingers, and as if he were the Pied Piper of Hamelin, the dogs followed him to the front of the ruin, where they, without giving us another glance, crept into the coolness of the shrubs.

'Betty!' The man yelled through a hole in the wall, 'we've guests,' and he disappeared inside.

On a small flagstone terrace, half-hidden under withered grass, we waited next to a table, - an old door on two trestles. Sam fell down on one of the creaky kitchen chairs, I also sat down and took the opportunity to ask after her ankle. She put her arm around my neck and kissed me.

'As long as the base is good, eh Sam,' I sighed.

The reasons for our disagreements were mainly stupid things. That she liked coffee, and I preferred afternoon tea; she hated smokers, and I preferred a joint to arouse sweet dreams; I loved food with a good splash of tabasco or spicy sauce, while that taste horrified her. Our main difference was that she wanted children and I didn't. I recently explained that my parents did not set the best example for me. Besides, I'm a teacher and spend enough time amongst teenagers. Nice, but am I glad I don't have to be a father to those youngsters. Sam was not satisfied with my argument. She needed a child!

As we were kissing away our afternoon bickering, the gypsy's English wife came out with an oil lamp. She introduced herself as Betty. Sheepishly I shook her hand. I mumbled my name and introduced Sam to her. In the weak light of the lamp, she looked about sixty. Her hair was dyed fiery red and hung untidily around her head; it was so thin that the skin of her skull shone through. Her braless breasts dangled under a stained sweater and her checked skirt was a bit twisted, with a bulging zipper on her stomach. She seemed to have painted her lips without a mirror.

She held a cigarette between her fingers. I looked closely at her and recognized beneath her shabby appearance a beauty that betrayed aristocratic elegance. Even her English resembled that of the Queen.

The man came out with a jug of urine-colored liquid and four glasses.

Sam asked for water. He went back inside and put a plastic cola bottle with water on the table. Greedy, we both gulped down a glass and waited.

Sam routinely started a conversation. I was bored and listened to her same stories, which I had heard so often: women's affairs and the weak sex: men!

The man, called Angel by Betty, came out again with a pan of fried sardines. 'Wine?' he asked. He took the jug and filled our water glasses to the brim.

Still thirsty, I took a big sip, just like Sam.

Angel asked what I was doing for a living.

'History teacher,' I replied shortly.

'Ha, muy interesante.' He sat down, rolled a cigarette, and gave a monologue about his life as a farmer. Then, with a meaningful grin, he said: 'But I used to do something completely else.'

I smiled a little as if I could understand what he was talking about and stared mesmerized at his fingers rolling the joint. I was longing for a draw.

Can you take us to our car?' I asked when I saw, in the flickering of the oil lamp, on Sam's watch that it was getting close to eleven.

'Si, si, of course. Mañana You can sleep here.'

That was a setback. Our stuff was in the car, and in the village, Camilla was waiting with food and a bed we had already paid for. We had to call her, but our mobile phones were in our backpacks. In the car.

I asked if Angel had a phone. 'Do you know La Parra's number?'

Once again, he ran inside and returned with a box full of cell phones and a flashlight. He held the light close to me when I tried one or two. Of course, they didn't work. The whole bunch of phones must have been stolen. Suddenly I decided to have some reservations about the couple. Though that was not easy, they took pleasure in their foreign guests, and the drinks flowed freely. Sam laughed an octave too high at Betty's stories, which I followed only indirectly, trying to concentrate on Angel's Spanglish. If Sam drank too much, she could become very unpleasant, and I could see the next morning already before me. Hangover time.

'Would you like to see the inn?' Angel pointed to the slanted door in the crumbled wall.

'Inn?'

'Yes, this building used to be a posada.'

'I can't imagine many people coming here,' I laughed.

'Five hundred years ago, yes, many people still lived here. Arabs.'

My interest was aroused. To prepare for this holiday, I

read a lot about Arab Spain between the eighth and fifteenth century. I also bored my students with my fascination and had asked them to write an essay about the differences in mentality between Islam and Christianity in Europe.

The first days of our holiday, when Sam melted on the beach in suntan lotion and extinguished her sand-breaded schnitzel body for seawater every hour, I sat in the shade of a palm tree engrossed in a book about the Reconquista. The Christians, Jews and Muslims co-existed relatively peacefully until the twelfth century. After that, Jews and Muslims were shamefully expelled and massacred by the Christians. Except in the province of Granada. In the Emirate of Granada, the Moors, as the Muslim population was popularly called, lasted another two hundred and fifty years, until 1492. This valley, Las Alpujarras, remained predominantly Arab until the end of the sixteenth century. Moorish guerrillas hid here and heroically opposed the Catholic converters. In the end, everyone had to convert to Christianity, or flee to Morocco. The more I read about it, the more that period intrigued me. I wanted to immerse myself in that interesting time and see the legacy of their buildings: The Alhambra in Granada, the Alcazar in Seville, and the mosque in Cordoba inside which the Christians in the sixteenth century had built a cathedral.

Angel refilled our glasses and stood up. Betty told how she came to Spain thirty years ago and worked as a nurse. Then she got to know him. She pointed her thumb at her partner and gave him a look as if she still regretted the day she'd ever met him. Sam was all ears; she barely noticed that Angel and I left, and went into the ruin. The smell of cat piss and cooking oil intoxicated me. It was pitch dark, and I almost tripped over a Great Dane. Angel turned on his flashlight just in time and grabbed my arm. Three kittens leapt like fleas, with their tail lifted, from between the dog's long legs and disappeared into the darkness. The animal raised its huge head and stared at me with eyes like sparkling beads. It was as if I looked straight into someone's soul, as if I was on the other side of his round pupil, and saw myself, but in another time. The magic of the moment broke as soon as the dog dropped its head with a soft thud, and a grunting sigh escaped its thin body.

A sonorous hum broke the silence, and a fluorescent light flickered on. Angel said: 'Solar energy, it always takes a while.'

The cold, white light slowly intensified and gave the space dimensions and contours. Some of the furniture broke free from the dark, like individuals introducing themselves. This was the couple's living area. Three kitchen chairs were arranged around a plastic table. In one corner, a two-burner gas stove balanced on a wooden crate. On top of it stood the greasy pan in which Angel had fried the sardines. In a rickety cabinet of stacked vegetable boxes were plates and glasses. I walked to a hole in the thick wall and saw thousands of stars twinkling in the sky. For a moment, I stepped back into my boyhood, when I had been given a kaleidoscope for my birthday.

Angel sat down at the kitchen table. He pulled a metal box towards him and gestured to the other chair. As soon as I sat down, a large brown and white pony walked past us. He neighed softly, and his mane danced around his neck as he moved his head. He left the room via another hole in the wall. Bewildered, I looked at Angel.

"That's Feliz. Has own way,' he said in a tone as if it wasn't strange at all that a horse was bantering through their living room. 'Kanuka?' Angel grinned.

A joint? I hadn't smoked marihuana in weeks, and suddenly, my mouth was watering. 'Yeah,' I laughed and relaxed. 'Let's smoke a joint.'

Angel got up and took a Moroccan water pipe with a blue glass vase from a niche in the wall. Even better, I thought. The water-cooled smoke always had a special effect on me, it was a deeper experience than just smoking a cigarette with some weed in it. I took some of the dried leaves between my fingers and sniffed a mild weed smell. 'What's this?' I asked, 'homegrown?' I didn't expect too much of it.

He nodded. 'Want a try?' He lit the stuff on the saucer at the top and sucked on the silver spout. 'It is Sage. I grow the plants myself and sell the dried leaves.'

'Sage? Ordinary sage?'

'No! Sage of the Ghosts. That's the best.'

As a teenager, I had experimented with all kinds of soft drugs, it was long ago, but I still remember the intense colors, the distinct taste in my mouth and that experience of weightlessness. Not averse to trying something new, I was keen to do this. Angel handed me the hose, and I sucked on the mouthpiece. Except for the bubbling water in the blue vase, it was dead silent. A black eye winked at me as I blew out the smoke. As if the air lifted me, I floated through space. After a few more puffs, my life looked rosy and carefree again. 'What a night,' I said to him in some language, Spanish? It was not English. I heard myself giggle. No idea how long it took, but slowly I came back to myself.

Angel was still sitting opposite me, looking at me seriously. There was a matchbox on the table in front of me. Where did that come from? Or had it been there all along? I couldn't remember. He pushed it towards me and gestured to look at it.

'Matches?' I said with a smile. I slid open the box and looked at a brown-green pasty gel. I sniffed it but I didn't smell anything. I pressed my index finger on it. It felt as if I was pushing into wet clay. I closed the box and gave it back to Angel.

'Try it.' He slid the box back to me. 'Now? What is it?'

'It's the herbal paste of Sage of the Ghosts,' Angel said solemnly as if it were royal jelly. 'You take some, let it melt on your tongue, and you will get in contact with another time. At least, if you're open to it. Then you will meet the truth.'

'What nonsense. Does such a thing exist? The truth.'

'Yes, of course, if you believe in it.' He said earnestly and looked at me faithfully. 'See what you want; either way, it will bring you something. I sometimes use it myself, and I'm back in time.' He stood up and reinforced his words with a sweeping gesture of both arms. 'This was once an old inn. We're in the taproom now.' He pointed to a corner. 'There's the bar. There, those crumbling steps lead upstairs to several rooms.'

I smiled at his fantasy and got an indignant look back. Apparently, we were both under the influence of the hookah and experienced some strange dream.

'Thanks to the Moors, this used to be a prosperous area. In this region people lived from silk cultivation. There are still a lot of mulberry trees in the area.' He handed me a glass of the strong wine and sat down again: 'When you said you are a historian, I immediately thought this is for you.' He pushed the matchbox back to me.

'No, thank you. I'm not in for dark experiments,' I said, trying to silence the curious whining voice in the back of my head.

'It's fantastic. The colors you see, the sounds you hear. You really experience that time.'

'Is it a sort of LSD?'

Angel shrugged.

I had used LSD when I was young and kept special memories of those experiences. I still saw myself hanging from the ceiling, thinking I was a bird. I would not mind having that sort of experience again.

'Something like that,' said Angel. 'But this stuff is much older and comes from nature. You can't say that about LSD. The Mexican Indians were already using this to generate prophetic visions.'

'How did you get it?'

Angel turned the matchbox around. 'In prison... when I met Betty.'

'Jail? Has she also been in jail?'

'Me yes. Not Betty. Didn't I say that before?'

I patiently listened to his story again. Twenty years ago, he was caught during a bank robbery in Granada. Shots were fired when he fled, and a bullet hit his lung. He was in the hospital for six weeks. There and then he met English Betty, a lovely blond nurse of forty-five. She had only just arrived in Spain and was on her own.

'I was twenty-five, and I thought she was hot, adventurous, and easy to lure in my nets, and she fell in love with me. That was good, because after the hospital I was in jail for eleven years; I needed someone who would look after me. Every month she would visit me wherever I was in jail. Zaragoza, Salamanca, Almería, those trips cost her a fortune. She taught me English, and when I got out, I stayed with her, but now she doesn't like Kama Sutra anymore.'

I listened to him with amusement; I didn't believe a word of his story. That broken English, that comical facial expression and his gestures were just laughable.

But Angel continued seriously: 'In prison, I met this Moroccan guy. Muhammad was convinced that he was a descendant of the Nasrid family. Rings a bell?'

I nodded. Of course, I knew the Nasrids. They were the last sultans of Granada who surrendered the Alhambra to the Catholic kings in 1492

'Betty nursed some old guy who owned this ruin. We were allowed to live here for free in exchange for supervision of the land and the harvest of olives and almonds. Muhammad was released shortly after me and came to visit us here. It was he who discovered the sage of the ghosts. It just grew along the edge of the water basin. Our first experiences were with the dried leaves. We've experimented a lot with it. It's great stuff.' Angel laughed, and I saw the caverns between his teeth. 'You are interested in the past. You have experience with mind altering drugs; I just saw that. You have a stable mind. You will love my herbal paste. Hombre, you have a great journey ahead of you.'

'I don't get it. What is this about?' I asked.

Angel shrugged. 'Here, have a piece. Nothing will happen to you.' He forced it on me, as if I was his guinea pig.

'No!' I jumped up. 'What if it is toxic or addictive?'

It isn't poison, but it could be addictive. The experience is addictive, anyway,' Angel said.

Mesmerized. I looked at the gel in the box with the color of baby poop. Did he speak the truth?

'How did Muhammad know about those herbs? And why don't you want to keep it?'

'I've plenty more. I sell the stuff.'

'How much?'

He shrugged, and I was tossed between wanting to try it or leaving the room right now, grabbing Sam, to walk back to our car, but I said: 'First I need to take a leak,' and stumbled through the dark to the rectangle that must be the outer door.

It must be well past midnight; the women were gone. A crescent moon stood in the inky sky above the faint profile of the Sierra Nevada, and a highway of stars floated above my head. I didn't notice the silence until a cicada chirped loudly in the tree above me. While peeing, I decided to just do it. I would ignore Sam's strict regime. I was on holiday. I was a free man. What harm could it do? Maybe a headache or some dizziness.

'Great, there you are.' Startled to hear Sam's voice, I peed all over my bare feet in the sandals. 'Betty made a bed for us. I'm diving in; are you coming too?'

I followed her to the side of the ruin. A streak of light from the oil lamp passed a door that creaked painfully as she pushed it open. In a bare room stood a dilapidated iron bed with a sheet. Sam's pupils were wide from the booze; she yawned and kicked off her slippers.

'How's your ankle, Squirrel?' I managed to ask, amazed at my presence of mind.

'Nags a bit, but luckily it's not too bad.' She slapped her hand next to her on the sheet that clearly others had slept on. Are you coming?'

'In a minute. I'm still chatting with Angel.'

Above her head, I saw a large stone-colored gecko against the rough wall. Its black eyes glittered and watched me closely. I forced myself to go to my girlfriend, and kissed her mouth from which came the stale smell of fried fish and wine. She threw her arms around my neck, but I pulled myself free. Just before I stepped back into the balmy night, the gecko disappeared into a hole in the wall. Then I knew for sure that I would take a trip with Angel's Sage of the Ghosts.

The Spanish farmer

I was intoxicated by the smell of weed when I returned. Angel sat with a joint at his kitchen table. He said, 'Betty has gone to bed.'

'Sam too.' I gave him a meaningful smile.

Apparently, he already knew the outcome of my short mission. Our eyes drifted to the matchbox in the middle of the table. He picked it up and offered it to me. Eager, I slid open the lid and pulled out a chunk that I rolled back and forth between my fingers.

'Put it under your tongue and let it dissolve slowly,' he instructed.

As I stared into his pitch-black pupils and saw the white stripe of the fluorescent light reflected in them, I did what he said. The stuff melted in my mouth and my tongue became heavy as if a dead animal was laying in my mouth. I felt like I was in a swimming pool, climbing a high diving board, and I shuffled to the very end with my eyes closed. I was in the middle of a universe. Around me was space, air and the smell, the smell... The thin board bent, I pushed off and took the plunge: into another time. But nothing happened, and I opened my eyes again. The taste on my tongue was stale, bitter, sour. And interesting.

'Don't you want some?' I asked automatically. My voice sounded far away.

Angel shook his head, emphatically. Why was he looking so intently into my eyes? I suddenly remembered the magnitude of my LSD trip twenty years ago, when I was floating through space but stayed within the confines of my head. The inside of my skull had been cloudless, like a blue sky. My temples acting as if they were the wings of a stage. As soon as the curtains were pulled open, I was blinded by luminous colors and bright light. I'd sat in the audience watching a stage performance and everything was so intense that the following days I found the world just a grey, dull affair. Would that happen to me now again? Would tomorrow, the light of the Andalusian sun appear less bright?

I chewed on my numb tongue, the feeling fascinated me, but nothing had changed. I opened my mouth to tell Angel, when a soft rhythmic murmur rang in my ears and the blood drained from my head. Someone swept up my brains with a dragnet, my eyes popped out, and something like ocean surf floated inside my head. At the same time, the murmur became a high-pitched buzzing. I pressed my palms to my ears and wanted to scream. Slowly the unbearable sound diminished, and it became a buzz.

A man stood in front of me, a colorful cloth ingeniously twisted around his head. My eyes adjusted to the dark. A few men sat on the floor, on carpets with bright patterns in green, red, and blue, as they were sucking on hookahs. I hardly discerned their figures in the haze of smoke. As soon as I moved my head, the carpets waved a little, they seemed to want to fly.

Behind the counter stood a heavy man wrapped in a leather apron. A dark beard hung under his chin, and heavy eyebrows leaned over his black eyes. A red turban adorned his head. I heard the clatter of tin plates and cups on stone. The man pushed a glass of tea towards me. The pure sound of a lute mingled with the tavern's buzz. The door swung open, and a young woman entered, holding a dead chicken in one hand.

I wanted to pick up the tea glass to take a sip, but the man next to me, wearing a white caftan, grabbed the glass and raised it to his lips.

'Hey, wasn't that my tea?' I uttered.

He turned away from me as if he hadn't heard me. But had he seen me? Why didn't these people react to me? I looked at my body. There was nothing Arabic about me. Brown legs protruded from ripped-off khaki pants, and golden hair shone on my calves. I recognized my feet in their worn sandals. Under my red-green striped T-shirt, I felt my ribs like the ripples of sand on a wet beach. My fingers slid up my neck, past my jaw. My little finger touched my earlobe with the golden ring I've worn since my recalcitrant teenage years. I had shaved this morning, but the bristly stubble on my cheek was poking through my skin again. My hand ran through my hair. Last week I had it cut short. It was still spiky as a bed of nails.

Sam liked to call me Prick, and I took the double meaning for granted. A strong smell drifted by. It was my own sweat from the past day. Never had I so consciously experienced my own body.

Behind me, the door was thrown open again, and I turned around.

A stocky man stepped inside. 'Salaam,' he said with one hand on his chest. He took in the space with narrowed eyes. He didn't look like the men around me. Instead, he seemed to be a Spanish farmer.

'Is there a room?' I heard the newcomer ask.

The innkeeper nodded. He walked ahead of the farmer up the stone steps, and they disappeared behind a green door. I followed them curiously. The farmer asked for oats and fresh water for his horse. 'We came from far,' he said.

'Of course,' replied the innkeeper. 'I'll take care of it right away.'

'I would like to eat something too.'

The innkeeper asked: 'You are not a Christian?'

'No, I'm a Muslim like you.'

'Why do you deny your origin?'

'Don't we all do that lately?'

'Not here. In our inn, we live with Allah.'

'Not much longer, I'm afraid. One day the Christians will also find you and force you to wear their garments and sing their songs, eat their food, and convert to their faith.'

'Won't go that far.' The innkeeper shook his head.

'Soon enough. You will die if you deny their orders, or you must flee. I am from Granada-town; we were all expelled there. Most of us fled to the other side, to Morocco.'

'But they've said we will live in peace, when we'll convert to Christianity.'

'They say so much. The Christian dogs know where to find us, and their revenge won't be sweet. They'll slaughter us to death.'

'The last sultan, you know, El Rey Chico, let us down.'

'Let us down?' The farmer's shapely eyebrows arched an inch.

'Yes, he betrayed us. He surrendered our people to the Catholic Monarchs without fighting for our cause.'

'He did what he could. But the sultan stood with his back against the wall. He negotiated and surrendered Granada to spare as many subjects as possible.' The peasant sounded stern; he defended the sultan.

The innkeeper asked boldly: 'How do you know?'

'I belong to his entourage.'

'Ah, so I have to be careful with what I say?' I saw a twinkle in the innkeeper's eyes.

The farmer stroked his eyes with a tired gesture, he shrugged as if it didn't matter anymore.

The innkeeper adjusted the bed mat, turned, and before

leaving the room, announced: 'In ten minutes, dinner will be ready.'

I snuck to the farmer and studied his face more closely. He had noble features, almost royal. A gloomy light shone in his dark eyes. He was about my age but well over a head shorter. A bright blue silk shirt with gold stitching on the collar shimmered beneath his coarse peasant smock. I raised my hand to feel the fabric but withdrew, startled, when he mumbled to himself: 'Mm, so that's what I did. I betrayed them. I knew it. I wasn't cut out for royalty; I'm not a fighter. What could I have done? It was written in the stars from the beginning.'

He did not feel my presence. Was I a nobody? I didn't exist, not in his time.

'By Allah, for decades, what am I saying, hundreds of years ago, when we Muslims stood together instead of fighting side by side for the same cause, our last hour had already come. It was only a matter of time, and I was the unfortunate one, the scapegoat, I had lost.'

The man spoke Arabic, but I just understood him anyway. How was this possible?

He went downstairs to the taproom and took a seat on a low bench at a rough wooden table. I sat opposite him with my legs crossed beneath me. The maid placed a tagine, filled with chunks of meat between golden yellow couscous in front of the man. He stared blankly ahead and ate little. I hoped he would start a conversation with another guest, but no one approached him, although the other men cast furtive glances in his direction.

Then he pushed the plate away, got up and walked out, into

the dark night. I followed him. The crescent moon shone brightly among the stars but gave little light. He went to the side of the inn, where the horses stood like dark shadows. His mount neighed softly when he stroked his neck. He released the animal from its burden, an elongated package. Carefully and respectfully, he tossed the bundle over his shoulder and quickly disappeared into the establishment. No one noticed him climbing the stone steps. I followed him closely with bated breath. In the room, he let the package slide onto the bed mat. Infinitely tender but with a haunted look, he unwrapped the contents from the rags.

Tense, I followed his movements and recoiled when I saw what emerged. It was a woman's body. And she was dead.

Softly, I heard the farmer's voice say: 'Our last journey together, Morayma, dearly beloved mother of my children. I will take you to Mondújar, where I will bury you next to your father and mother. Our tragic and miserable life together has come to an end; what remains for me is the memory of our happy moments. Your eyes, your mouth, your smile, your delicate skin... , and your tears.'

She was irretrievably dead but opened her eyes at the sound of her name. I crawled out of the shadows and squatted down next to the man and bent over her, together with him. As one person, we stared into her deep blue eyes. His tears dripped onto her dress.

Then, her brittle voice sounded: 'My love, my king, weep not. It was I who made you unhappy. Go and live in freedom.' The words left her mouth without moving her lips.

He kissed her. His wet cheeks rubbed against her translucent wax skin.

Embarrassed and moved, I withdrew a little.

He lifted a glittering black stone from her chest and weighed it in his hand.

'Take it, the black diamond, your wedding present to me,' she said. 'The precious proof of the power of the Nasrids. Hide the diamond so it will never be found again.'

Carefully, the man unhooked the thick gold chain around her neck and let it swing, like a pendulum, between his and my eyes. In the dim light, I saw a strange glow in the gleaming black of the heavy stone. The man got up quietly, his eyes wandering over the rough stone wall. At eye level, he pulled out a large chunk of a rock. Grit and clay rattled to the ground.

He released the black diamond from the chain and put it in his pocket. He briefly raised the stone to his lips, then pushed the diamond deep into the wall's hole.

My gaze flew back and forth between Morayma's dead eyes and the man's actions. He mortared the fallen stones back with the grit, clay, and water from the carafe in the corner. Soon there was nothing left to see on the rough wall. He spread the rest of the sand with his boot on the already filthy floor.

The man knelt again next to his wife, took her in his arms and rocked her lovingly from side to side. Mesmerized, I looked into her vacant look and tried to name the color of those eyes: forget-me-not, a cloudless sky... I ran my fingers over the fabric of her robe. My breath touched her white dead skin, etching that intense blue color into my memory. For a moment, I closed my eyes. I wanted to lay my weary head on her chest like a child does to its mother.

She moved. Startled, I lifted my head, and felt my leaden eyelids. I looked into two green eyes. Green eyes with brown dots.

'Jacob, what are you doing?'

'Sam?'

Propped up on her elbows, my girlfriend stared at me. Where was Morayma? By shaking my head, the images disappeared; they hid somewhere in the wings of the stage.

'You're so heavy. Why the interest? Have you never seen me sleeping?' snapped Sam.

'Honey, I'm sorry. I wanted to check your watch for the time.' It was my voice, but I had no idea what part of my brain produced that phrase.

'A quarter past six,' she said, holding her wrist in front of her face. 'Did you sleep?'

'Yes, Yes. I'm going outside for a while. Watching the sunrise.' Dizzy and nauseous, I staggered away from her. Outdoors, the silence fell over me. There was no inn at all. There were no horses. This was the ruin where we had been lavishly received the previous evening by that odd couple. On the shadowy shape of the table stood the empty carafe, a full ashtray, and the leftovers on our plates were eaten by the cats. I propped up a fallen kitchen chair and made my way to the east side of the ruin. I must have dreamed. I had fallen asleep under Angel's eyes, and he had put me in bed next to Sam.

Between the clumps of grass, I sank into a meditative posture I knew so well from the many Buddhas my mother collected. With my eyes closed, I tried to retrieve the jumbled images of the couple in the inn. I couldn't. I collapsed and fell forward, exhausted, with my head in a thyme bush. When I half straightened up again, I was kneeling like an old Mohammedan with my face turned to the east. In the distance, the sky started to brighten already.

A wet tongue in my face woke me up. I peeked through my eyelashes and saw four dogs panting above me, ready to pounce on me. Their drool dripped onto my chest. I pretended to be asleep and said to myself: 'Jacob, those beasts don't do anything. Have faith.' I held out a hand and petted the closest one. I worked myself up on my elbows until I was seated. The warmth of the sun touched my face. I rubbed my eyes, which felt thick and watery. Above my head, the beautiful birds swarmed again. A cicada gently began its morning chirp in the olive tree next to me.

Angel stood by the table, saw me wake up, raised his hand, and headed for me.

I was back in reality.

'And?' he asked curiously. 'Was the trip worth it?'

Pleased with his interest, I immediately said: 'I was at the inn and saw the Arabs.'

Angel's gaze drifted to the sky. With his hand over his eyes, he followed the birds that circled over our heads, making that thin clunking sound.

'What are those, Angel?' I rose, stretching my stiff limbs and blinked in the bright morning light. Their yellow collars glittered as if they were golden.

'Bee-eaters. Aren't they beautiful? Blue, yellow, brown, red, they have all the colors of the rainbow.'

'Yes, very special and so many.'

'In the morning, they gather above the valley. They hunt

insects all day and come back just before sunset.'

'Angel, I saw an Arab, dressed as a peasant, with a dead woman tied to his horse. She had blue eyes.'

His gaze left the sky, rested on my face for a moment, uncomprehending, and then wandered away again. How different he was last night. Then, I thought we were friends. Now, on this new day, none of our closeness was left. Something that looked like friendship no longer existed. His wandering gaze made me think as if he wanted to get rid of us quickly.

Just to say something, I asked: 'How much does that stuff cost?'

'Oh, you want to try it again?' Angel grinned.

'Yeah, it was fascinating. That farmer hid a black stone. A diamond. Somewhere in the ruin here.'

'How do you mean?'

'That man last night was definitely important. His wife wore a black diamond around her neck. The power of the Nasrids, she called it. She wanted him to hide the stone.'

'Black diamond, you say?' I nodded.

'There is an old Arabic legend about the black diamond. That is why the Moors would have stayed in La Alpujarra for so long. They were looking for the sacred stone, which once fell from heaven and gave the power of Allah to Granada,' said Angel.

'I saw that man hiding the diamond. Here, in the wall of the room above.'

He looked at me incredulously, shrugged and smiled. 'There are so many legends about the Moriscos. No one knows what's true.' Sunlight fell on the chipped teeth in his mouth. Angel had been a heavy user, or maybe he still was?

Was it wise to get involved with him and his hallucinogenic stuff? I wanted to ask more questions, but he turned away and walked to the table where Betty and Sam sat chatting. I simply could not share my enthusiasm with him. Betty poured me tea from a dented enamel teapot. I needed coffee, but I had to make do with a cup of lukewarm ditch water. I dipped a piece of bread in it and sucked like a baby without teeth.

With my senses still on edge, I smelled a strong scent. I couldn't imagine Angel drinking tea. Then, I saw the golden color in his glass. The guy drank brandy. I smiled behind my hand; what a life here.

After breakfast, Betty hugged us and said: 'You're always welcome.' We nodded our thanks. Knowing we would never see them again.

Via a narrow donkey trail, Angel took us to the car. The heat was already like a quilted blanket between the rock walls. The gypsy, with one lung and already some alcohol in his blood, walked steadily upwards. Sam followed on her slippers, dodging the loose stones. I came ten yards behind her with heavy legs, panting like a pack mule.

At the car, Sam got behind the wheel, waving to Angel with a distant glance. She started the engine. I shook his hand and thanked him for the hospitality. He grabbed my shoulders and hugged me the way I'd seen Andalusian men do. I stood stunned in his arms while he slid the matchbox into my hand.

'Here,' he said. 'Buy it from me!'

'But I don't want it.'

'Yes, take it. A hundred euros.'

'I look at him, wondering.' I watched Sam, who waited impatiently behind the wheel. I hastily opened the trunk and got my old grey backpack, found my wallet, and gave him two fifty-euro bills.

'Great, thank you,' Angel said. 'One last warning! Be careful with it. Never use it when you are alone. Don't walk around during a trip; sit in one place. And take it when it is dark; that gives you the best experience.'

With mixed feelings and afraid of Sam's eagle eyes, I quickly slipped the box into my backpack.

La Parra in Aireluz

Sam drove too fast around a bend and almost landed in the ravine next to the road.

'Switch back to second gear.' I couldn't resist saying.

'Are you driving, or am I?'

'You are, and I am suggesting something useful.'

Her devilish look silenced me; all my words would add fuel to the fire. Ignoring her clumsy driving, I turned my attention to the hills to our left, below the road. The rocks glowed reddish copper and sienna brown in the morning light. My irritation soon subsided because, one by one, the images from last night crawled out of the stage's wings. They were sharply outlined behind my eyelids. I was back at the inn. The devotion the man showed as he unwrapped his dead wife had touched me deeply. I swallowed and swallowed and cleared my throat. I felt a kind of responsibility for that royal couple. Strange, it had been a fantasy, a hallucination caused by the stuff from that matchbox. But I couldn't ignore my emotions.

'Beautiful here, isn't it?' I heard Sam say next to me.

'Yes.'

'Is that all? Have you got nothing to say about last night?'

'Last night?' I tore myself from my thoughts. 'Nice couple.'

'Well, tell me. That guy, Angel, is something! Betty told me stories about him. You don't want to know what a life those two have together. And yet she stays with him.'

'She probably has nowhere to go,' I muttered.

'You seemed pretty close to him.' She glanced at me. 'You were smoking weed, weren't you? Betty said he grows a certain kind of salvia and puts it in a water pipe. I bet you have a pounding headache because of it.'

'Salvia yes. Sage, the kitchen herb,' I uttered. That's what he called the paste: Sage of the ghosts? Did he give me that? Did I pay a hundred quid for a bunch of kitchen herbs?

'Yes, it was exceptional. You should try... Oh no,' I sneered, 'that is too much off the beaten track of your middle-class life.'

Sam raised her brows and said sweetly: 'Darling, you know I don't smoke, and I wish you didn't either. It's bad for you.' She started a new intimidation tactic. I didn't have much energy to fight her, so I kept my mouth, but I said: 'Bad? It is otherwise available at the pharmacy.'

'Bullshit. For pain relief, yes. But it makes you sluggish, forgetful, absent. I don't recognize you anymore, and you live in a world of your own. When you're stoned, I can't get close to you.'

This point she'd raised a little too often. If I smoked a joint, she couldn't control me, and that's what she didn't like. Too bad for her. This was one of the last things I had for myself; I wouldn't want to be made into the drowsy fool her father was.

'Come on, Squirrel, the sun is shining. We are on holiday, driving through the Sierra Nevada, one of the most beautiful landscapes in Europe, and you are talking about smoking pot. Let's enjoy and not argue.' I was proud of the calmness in my voice because I felt something nasty bubbling up.

I'm not arguing,' she said sweetly. 'I'm just stating the obvious, but you can't stand criticism.'

'For goodness sake. Shut up.' There it was. Like a tidal wave, the rage swept through my body to my head. I couldn't take it anymore; I was utterly done with that eternal patronizing and know-better. Damn, this nonsense would ruin our entire day. What? The whole holiday.

Thank God, Sam kept her mouth shut. Without a word, she drove into a white village. She slammed the brakes for a tight passage between two houses, narrowly missing the tail of a skinny dog that lay in a streak of shadow along a facade. We drove to the church and Sam parked on a square next to a few other cars. We got out. She pushed her sunglasses into her hair, opened the trunk and grabbed her camera bag. Within seconds, she started clicking. I also grabbed my backpack and hid the matchbox in a secret pocket behind the zipper. I had already decided, I wanted to make another trip to the past. Not yet knowing when, but I definitely wanted to relive the experience. Addictive or not.

We strolled through the village, looking for La Parra, the Bed & Breakfast of Sam's friend, Camilla.

'This is an original Moorish village,' I said. The whitewashed houses leaned organically against each other along steep streets; the chimneys on the flat roofs were round and made me think of mushrooms with their large flat slates on top. Below us, we saw tomatoes drying on a roof and strands of fiery red peppers hung on a facade. Geraniums in pots bloomed lushly. A bougainvillea in smashing pink, and scented jasmine trailed along the railing of a balcony. A traditional farmer, walking beside his mule, approached. The animal's flanks were covered with bunches of corn leaves, dancing to the rhythm of its step. Sam asked if she could take pictures. The man gave her a broad smile and proudly posed next to his mule.

Under a discolored beer sign I saw a door with sticky chains to keep the flies outside. Behind it, pub noises could be heard. I peeked into a dark, smoky room as if I stepped back into my hallucination from last night and I became aware that my meeting with the Moor and his wife slumbered perpetually in the back of my mind.

'They probably know where La Parra is.' I said over my shoulder to Sam and stepped inside. An old fan blew some air around. Three men with weather-beaten faces were talking loudly and interrupted their conversation to glance at us.

'Hola,' I shouted cheerfully.

'Hola,' they replied and turned to each other again.

'Cafe solo,' I ordered from the man behind the counter. I longed for a burst of energy.

'Cerveza y tapas,' Sam said, and to me: 'I'd die for a cold

beer and tapas.' She pointed at the saucers next to the men's glasses, on which something indefinable was visible.

The bartender nodded, and a moment later, Sam gulped down her cold beer and picked at the tentacles of fried squids.

'Don't you want something to eat?'

'No, I'll stick to coffee.' I couldn't even think about food, even though I hadn't had breakfast and, apart from Angel's few sardines and bits of sausage, I had also skipped dinner.

'Well, I do; I'm starving. Look... ' Sam pointed to the blackboard behind the bar: 'Menu del día: ten euros. Shall we eat here later?'

When she paid, Sam asked about Camilla and the Bed & Breakfast. The bartender nodded and pointed out La Parra, it was close by; we couldn't miss it.

Outside, the heat fell on us as if we'd entered an oven. 'How do these people function here?' Sam said.

'Not.' I muttered.

Around the corner, Camilla was sweeping the street.

'Hey, hi, Sam, I was expecting you yesterday,' Camilla greeted us in an easy-go-lucky way I instantly liked.

''That's right.' In the blink of an eye, Sam explained our adventure with Angel and Betty. I was amazed. I would have gone into much more detail; as a teacher, I even was told that I was too wordy. In the meantime, I waited behind Sam for Camilla to greet me too.

I had met her once at Sam's birthday party.

'Hi Camilla. How do you like living here?' I asked, and took her hand, but she gave me a kiss.

'I live in paradise.'

'Jacob, will you get our suitcases from the car?' Sam gestured over her shoulder and followed Camilla inside. Camilla muttered something about 'heat and flies' and closed the door in front of me. Confused, I trudged down the empty street to our car, which had been parked in the sun and had turned into an oven. Slightly numb, I dragged our travel bags to the Bed & Breakfast.

Sam and Camilla were chatting in the hall, and as soon as I entered, Camilla led the way to our room.

Like a mule, I carried the luggage upstairs.

'Do feel at home. 'Mi casa, es tu casa.' Camilla gestured broadly. 'Come down and have a drink when you want and sit in the shade,' she added, and left us alone.

'Maybe we won't have to pay for last night,' I said, stretching lazily on the bed, which was noticeably narrower than our bed at home.

'But of course we will. I'm going to take a shower; I feel like a sweaty mop.' Sam disappeared into the bathroom.

'Sure, we will,' I muttered, and fell asleep.

Sam woke me barely half an hour later. 'The food is good in that local pub, Camilla said. Carmen is an excellent cook. Hurry up, dude, the kitchen is open between two and four, and it's already three o'clock.'

Cazon Morayma

*T*he dining room next to the bar was packed.

'Where do all these people come from in this dead quiet

village?' I thought aloud.

'Really an away from home dining culture here.' Sam pointed to a two-person table in the corner beneath a loudly blaring television. 'And always indoors because it's too hot outside.'

My girlfriend was in her element. She loved food, and as an editor of the recipe magazine 'Kitchen Hands', she always looked for tasty dishes.

'Yum, I really enjoy this local food; so honest and fresh.' She picked up the menu and read aloud: 'Menu del día. First, Gazpacho, that's a cold tomato soup. Then we can choose albondijas, lomo, cordero, alas de pollo. This is all meat, or do you prefer fish? Calamares, boquerones, sardines fritos, bacalao.'

I had no clue what it all meant, but I nodded: 'Okay, I'll have fish.' I still wasn't hungry, but at least fish was easy to digest.

'This is a la carte, which is a lot more expensive. Here, pescado: Caballa en salsa verde, Gamba's pil pil, Cazon Morayma...'

I sat up straight. 'Cazon Morayma? I would like that.'

'Do you know what it is?'

'No clue, but it sounds nice.'

'Good, I'll have cordero, lamb chops.'

A girl came to take our order and greeted us: 'Good afternoon.'

Apparently, she wanted to unleash her five words of school English on us, so I asked: 'Who was Morayma?'

'No tengo idea, I'll ask mi madre.'

The mother turned out to be the cook, Carmen. She came

to our table, wearing a clean apron and a white cap on her dyed hair. 'No hay Cazon Morayma,' she said.

'What does that mean?' I asked.

'She doesn't have your dish,' Sam translated.

'What a pity. But who was it?'

'What's he saying?' Carmen looked at my girlfriend, ignoring my presence. 'Who was Morayma?' Sam asked in her best Spanish.

'Cazon? Pez blanco, muy suave?'

'Si, si, a white fish, but who was Morayma?' I asked emphatically now. 'La esposa de Boabdil,' said the cook.

'B o a b d i l's wife?' I consciously tasted every letter of that name. Boabdil.

'Si! El ultimo sultan del Granada.' The woman turned to another table where she began a chat with two men.

'The last sultan of Granada?' asked Sam. 'Where do you get that from?'

'She just told us.'

'And what about this, uh... Morama?'

'Morayma! I don't know, but 1492 was the dramatic turning point in Spanish history. The last sultan of Granada, Muhammed Abu Abdallah, nicknamed Boabdil, surrendered his emirate on January 2nd to Ferdinand and Isabella, the Catholic Monarchs.' I saw Sam's eyes turn listlessly, and I shut my mouth. Of course, I had read something about Boabdil, but I had never heard his wife's name: Morayma. However, last night I had seen her. In real life. I had to ask the cook why there was a dish on the menu with Morayma's name. Why did someone name a fish dish after the wife of the last sultan?

Carmen turned back to us and asked what I wanted to eat. I stumbled, 'Por que...' This was not the right time for my question, and I said in a grave voice: 'Boquerones.'

Sam looked at me with raised eyebrows. 'What is the matter with you? First, you don't want to eat anything, then you choose an obscure dish, and you're disappointed when it isn't available, and to top it off you choose fried anchovies, which you never have liked.'

I shrugged. Could I tell her that I had met Boabdil and Morayma? No, of course not. But she was my girlfriend. I shared my life with her. My head was full of it, and the confrontation with this dish couldn't be a coincidence.

'Sam,' I began. 'I have to tell you something.'

'What about? Do you want to leave me? Is there someone else?'

It was meant as a joke, but it sounded serious and annoyed me. 'God, please don't always fill it in your way.'

'What else can I make of it? You look like you just swallowed an earwig.'

Despite my mood, I smiled; damn, that's how I felt. 'Last night, I experienced something with Angel. You'll never believe it, but I've gone back more than five hundred years.'

'Pooh, no, I don't believe that. Is that what that sage does? Betty said he sells the junk for a lot of money.'

The waitress placed a salad dish, a basket with bread, a bottle of water and a pitcher of wine on the table. Her strong armpit odor wafted by, my stomach turned. Sam immediately skewered an olive on her fork and said, chewing: 'Delicious olives.' She lifted the pitcher. 'Wine?'

I searched for the right words, ignoring the alarm bell

about what Sam had heard from Betty. I wanted to tell my girlfriend about my experience, but she was not interested. I tried again: 'You know, last night I met someone. Someone I felt connected to as if it was someone... Someone like me.'

'You mean Angel?' With her mouth full, she pointed her fork at me and pushed back her sunglasses with the other hand. 'I don't hope so.'

'No, no, Angel's got nothing to do with it.'

'But you were sitting together at that kitchen table, I saw you.'

That was true. Would I have seen Boabdil in Angel and Morayma in Betty or Sam? That thought confused me.

'No, really, there was someone else; I fused with that other person. Our feeling and thinking, we were one, a unity. Together one. I was someone else, but myself simultaneously, and yet I wasn't. It was an incredible feeling.'

'Well, honey,' Sam put the back of her hand theatrically on my forehead, 'there are pills for these kinds of aberrations. I think you got a sunstroke.'

I shuddered under her hand. I wanted to say that I had been in contact with myself in a special way for the first time. She liked to dive into psychology, but I saw the girl approaching with our plates. Sam got a plate full of crispy lamb chops while I stared at the dead eyes of a dozen fried anchovies.

Until well after dark, we lingered in the garden of La Parra. Camilla came out with candles and more wine. Sam talked tirelessly with her friend and the other guests; I kept aloof and went upstairs to our bedroom. In Camilla's bookcase I found 'The Ornament of the World' by Rosa Menocal, a book which covered, among other things, the culture and literature of the time in Arab Spain, named: El Andalus. I read and made notes in my diary.

A few hours later, slightly tipsy, Sam crawled next to me, woke me from a deep sleep and accidentally hit my face.

'Stupid, look out. Why always so rude?' I snapped.

'Sorry,' she giggled.

I threw off the sheet and jumped out of bed. I'm going to sleep somewhere else.'

'Good luck, the bed & breakfast is full. Sleep in the bathtub.'

'Why are you so unkind?' I asked, aggrieved.

'Who's unkind? Well?'

'I don't want to lie next to a drunk.'

'Don't yell like that.'

'You are the one screaming!'

The old singsong. We had a fight about nothing. Sam turned around and immediately fell asleep. I lay down on the edge of the narrow bed, with the feeling there was an imaginary bag of ice between us. Wide awake, I listened to her snoring and finally dozed off into a nagging half-sleep.

During breakfast, Sam apologised for her rude behavior: 'In my normal rhythm of work and enough sleep, I can manage my hormones well. You know that Jacob, you hardly notice my whims. But now we're on holiday. We eat differently and at irregular times, and last night, I hardly slept, so I have it more serious. I'm sorry.'

I swallowed. There it was. Normally, I kept track of her hormonal moods, but last night I'd forgotten. I wrote her menstrual periods in my diary, so I knew approximately when her egg burst. I got that from a colleague. Once I read big and thick underlined P.M.S. in his diary, I asked: 'What's that?'

Rolling his eyes, he began to lament about his wife. 'Pre-Menstrual Syndrome? Criminal, that's what it is. One week a month, I have no life.'

I suddenly realised that Sam also struggled with something like this. Just before her ovulation, she could get into a rotten mood that would drive any man crazy, headache, depression, and extremely touchy. During her period, everything seemed to be forgotten and forgiven, and the quarrels were settled again and everything was okay. Some days were worse than others, so I didn't always notice it, but since I wrote down 'P.O.S.' in my calendar around her bad days, our relationship had suddenly improved.

I squeezed her hand for a moment. 'Glad you said so, Squirrel. Last night I forgot your P.O.S. So, from now on, we will have fun together again?'

'We're going to have a good time, Prick.' She hugged and kissed me, brushed my hair the wrong way and gave me the sweetest smile.

'I hope so,' I sighed. The capriciousness of the female sex continued to amaze me.

Of course, I understood what that smile meant. My wife wanted a child, and for the next few days, she was susceptible to conception. Three months ago, she had her IUD removed, against my will. And now, I realised that her present ovulation syndrome was more severe than ever. I had to be careful, at this time of the month and wouldn't buy into her advances. No sex for me, this week.

'Okay, what are the plans for today?' I asked matter-of-factly. 'Granada, right? Tomorrow we have tickets to the Alhambra.'

'Yes, of course, the Alhambra.' How could I have forgotten, the highlight of our trip, I was very much looking forward to.

'Actually, I don't know if I'm in the mood for that,' Sam began. 'It seems to be quite touristy, according to Camilla. Can't we skip it and stay here for a few more days?'

'What? We're not going to change plans, are we? We can see through those tourists. It's really special, you know. It'll be super nice, and I invite you for a nice meal at the Parador.'

She gave in, hesitantly, though. I smiled. I knew how to placate her.

After breakfast, Camilla waved us goodbye.

'We'll be back for sure,' Sam cried.

'Do. And when I'm in the UK, I'll drop by.'

'Nice, the coffee will be ready,' Sam echoed through the street.

The grey head of a neighbor in a black dress appeared in front of a window, watching us walk past.

'Have a good trip; it was nice having you here,' Camilla called out and started muttering to the neighbor in Spanish.

The village life was in full swing. A white van with *Pescado Moreno* on the side, drove by honking loudly to the square near the church. Two women dressed in black with floral aprons swept their doorsteps. A man on a mule trudged out of the village, a long-eared dog sat in front, and a water bottle dangled from the animal's withers. The church clock struck eleven.

The fishmonger had parked next to our car. Between a pair of grey heads, I recognized Carmen, the cook at the restaurant. I also peeked in the car at the sardines, the tank of slippery squid, mussels, king prawns, and a few more fish I wasn't familiar with.

The Moor's Last Sigh

'Just let us listen to the silence,' I said after a good hour of driving. I stopped in a parking lot along the road and got out. While stretching my legs, I heard a mountain stream crashing from the rocks. 'Weird, it's so dry here; where's that water coming from?' I asked.

'Camilla talked about that,' Sam said. 'The water comes from springs high in the mountains and runs down via irrigation canals. It's water for their crops. Throughout the Sierra Nevada is a network of canals, and each farmer has water at a certain time.'

'You're right. I read about that. In the past, the Arabs built those canals. They open the canal to allow the water to enter their fields, and after a certain time, they close them again.'

'These channels are called 'Acequias', there is a guard appointed to make sure no one steals water. Water equals gold here, Camilla said.'

'I love that, life is so simple here, and the peace is so beautiful.' We hung over the wooden railing above the ravine. I focused on the undulating hills in front of us, covered with a patchwork of colors; orchards, gleaming water basins and, in the distance, walls of eroded rocks.

'Would you like to live here?' Sam looked at me sharply from the side. 'I wouldn't! Way too quiet. You would bury me alive. Camilla told me about her kind of life. Just imagine, she had a career in broadcasting and lived in a posh neighborhood in London. And yet she finds her happiness here in the sticks.'

'I certainly could imagine a life like that. No distraction by things that seem important but do not yield anything.'

'Such as?'

'Running around, standing in traffic jams, busy with making and spending money because the world you live in demands that.'

'But you don't live in such a world, do you?'

'I try to avoid it, by cycling to school; you often say that I'm antisocial, and you know how much I hate shopping malls.'

'It's easy to talk like that, since I do the shopping.'

'That is not what I mean. You know what I'm talking about.'

'Yes, but it's still nice to have enough money, and we are able to do what we want. We are very well off with two incomes.'

There was something familiar above my head. I stared into the sky and heard that clucking sound. 'Listen, there are those birds again. They are bee-eaters, Angel said.'

'If only you were such a bird, right? You could fly away into the past when it gets too difficult in the present.' Sam pegged my side as we walked back to the car and got behind the wheel. I walked in silence to the passenger side. Sitting next to her, I studied her profile, that firm, determined chin suddenly annoyed me. And what did she mean by that comment about flying away? Had she listened at all during lunch yesterday?

We drove further west, through the high Alpujarras and white authentic Moorish villages to Trevélez. A little over a thousand bends away lay Pampaneira, Capileira and Bubion, three mountain villages overshadowed by the two highest peaks of the Iberian Peninsula: the Mulhacén and the Veleta. Photos usually showed them shrouded in a thick layer of snow, but now, in summer, the behemoths stared down at us, dry and barren.

We stopped for a coffee. Under a huge plane tree, we found a shaded spot on a terrace strewn with red plastic tables and unoccupied chairs.

'August, and no tourists here?' Sam said. 'How do these people earn a living?'

We placed an order, and I took the travel guide from my backpack. While we waited for our coffee, I summarized the history of Las Alpujarras for Sam. 'So, after 1492, the rebels, the Muslims who revolted against the Christians, were hiding here. They were given a choice: either leave for Morocco or convert to Christianity. The ones that converted were called Moriscos, Moors, but secretly they remained faithful to Allah.'

'What a situation,' Sam said.

Someone brought the coffee, Sam paid and put the change back in our household purse.

I took the first sip and burned my tongue. Picking up the guidebook again, I ran my tormented tongue across my palate and said: 'Listen, this really happened here in Las Alpujarras. In 1567, Philip the II forbade the Arabs to speak their own language. They were no longer allowed to dress in Arabic style; their bathing rituals, chants, prayers, and eating habits, nothing was tolerated by the Christians. Here in this valley, there was a revolt led by a certain Don Fernando, a Christian Moor who called himself Aben Humeya. North African Muslims, the Berbers, came to his aid. Then Aben Humeya was murdered by his own people, his cousin Aben Abu succeeded him, and they stabbed him to death too. It was an extremely bloody and grim time; Around 1575 the guerrilla struggle against Christian authority, was definitively over.'

'Hardly five centuries ago,' Sam said.

'Exactly, that's why you can still feel the Arab atmosphere in these villages. But listen, this is also interesting.' I took the last sip of the lukewarm coffee and read: 'By the end of the fifteenth century, almost the entire originally Arab population had been deported to other parts of Spain. Some men and women were even given to the royalty in Portugal and other parts of Europe. And poor peasant families from Galicia and Asturias in northern Spain were brought to this area. In each village, though, one Moorish family had to stay. They had to pass on their knowledge of sericulture and agriculture, and the irrigation systems to the next generations. But finally, they cultivated more grain products, and sericulture became less important. This whole migration marked the beginning of the decline of Las Alpujarras.'

'Crazy idea that it all seems such a short time ago,' Sam reiterated.

'Every year, many villages still celebrate the battle between the Moors and the Christians. Half the villagers dress up as a Moor in white and the other half play a Christian. In the village square, they harass each other on horseback and shoot with blanks.'

'Nice, can we see that?'

'Didn't we pass through the village of Valor earlier today? The fiesta is held there in mid September.'

'Then we're a few weeks too early. Unfortunately.'

By lunchtime, we left the valley and drove north onto the highway between Motril and Granada.

'El ultimo Suspiro del Moro,' Sam read aloud at the next exit. 'That means the Moor's last sigh, isn't it?' She was glad to recognize some of the Spanish she'd learned.

I nodded. 'That last Moor was the sultan, Boabdil.' On the opposite side of the highway a hotel had his name written on the facade. 'Let's have lunch there.' Strangely, I was not hungry, while generally, I used to eat like a horse. But I was just curious about this place. What would happen if I took some of Angel's Sage right here? I thought 'paste' was too prosaic a name for this hallucinatory product. Sage sounded much better; it also rang like age. Could I get back to Boabdil again, in his time?

At the reception desk, I picked up a brochure. Sam looked for a table by the window, and I went to the toilet. In the bathroom, I dug up the matchbox from my backpack and examined it closely in the bright light. It was an old matchbox; the picture had weathered, and the letters were worn. I decided to buy a nice sturdy box for it somewhere.

Would it be wise to take a bit now? Suppose I acted weird, and Sam would ask questions? On the other hand, from her reaction to my behavior I could better understand what happened during a trip and how my body behaved when my mind wasn't in it.

I plucked some crumbs of the sage, no more than a few grains like coarse salt, rolled it into a little ball and stuck it under my tongue. Without waiting to see what happened to me, I walked to the dining room. Traffic roared down the highway below us. On the other side, the Sierra Nevada lay like a massive clump in the blistering midday heat. I sat across from my girlfriend and put the leaflet on the table in front of me.

'Here, along this highway, is the rock on which Boabdil once sank and wiped away some tears.' I tapped my finger on the leaflet and pointed outside. 'The last sultan had been expelled from Granada and was with his family exiled to La Alpujarra. At this rock, he would have heaved a deep sigh, sobbing: "Goodbye beloved Alhambra, goodbye Granada".'

Sam grabbed the folder. 'Yesterday, Carmen, the cook at the restaurant, was talking about Boabdil and his wife, um... Mora, or something like it? Here...' She read aloud: 'Oh no, it was his mother who said this to him: "Son, you cry like a child, for what you could not defend as a man." That seemed a rather harsh correction. What had he done wrong?'

'He surrendered his beloved kingdom of Granada to the Catholic Monarchs. His people, especially his mother, did not thank him for that.'

She laughed: 'What mother says these things to a son, and then is still portrayed like that five hundred years later. So,

I may presume mother was wearing the pants and son was the weakling?'

'Maybe he was weak, yes. That is how it is written in the history books: He was a fat and spoiled brat. Personally, I think he was more a puppet of the system, as national administrators often are.'

'What's so interesting about him?'

'I don't know. He fascinates me, his story, the family intrigue, but also the psychology of how he was used, set up. You know, I'm a history freak; that's my job.' I gave her a weak smile and tried to feel if anything changed in me. Was I traveling to the past?

Sam nodded at the waiter who was looking our way and said: 'Do you recognize something in him? Your mother was also dominant in your life.'

'Inez? Why do you come up with her?'

'Well, you oh, I just thought... when she once said...'

'... Jacob is also such a weakling,' I finished her sentence.

'I'm not saying that.' She smiled at me forgivably.

I saw her thinking, and she had no idea how she insulted me. She thought I was her possession, which gave her a license to find things about me and decide for me. Still. With trembling fingers, I put the leaflet in my backpack and felt the square box. The sage didn't work. I probably didn't take enough.

The waiter brought the menu, which Sam studied hungrily. 'What do you want, honey? Meatballs in tomato sauce, omelet, squid...'

Without understanding those words, I interrupted halfway through her summary, while black spots danced before my eyes: 'Yeah, I'll have a tortilla.'

I tried to focus on the mountains beyond the window. What a magical view. Crazy, those mountain peaks were wearing a white hat? Snow? No, they were barren and dry before. Something moved on the white slope. I saw a long row of black figures creeping up; they looked like ants. Did I see what I thought I saw, or did I want to see what I saw? I narrowed my eyes. What happened there? I had read that the old king, Boabdil's father, Muley Hasan, was buried on the highest peak of the Sierra Nevada. Did this look like a funeral procession? Was this his Moorish funeral? The king was buried in the ice of the Mulhacén, and Boabdil? Was he there at that moment? He and his father didn't have a good relationship. Boabdil's mother, Aisha, had set up her son against his father. That was the beginning of the end. The old king refused to pay taxes to Ferdinand and Isabella and thereby lost the confidence of his own people. He was a heartless and obstinate man, so I had understood.

A current of air swept past me, and a hand placed a plate with a shiny yellow island in front of me. My tortilla. On Sam's plate lay a variety of meat: chorizo, black pudding, ham, and a fried egg.

The cool country wine had a sweet sherry taste and lubricated my throat and numbed my tongue, which was still hurting from the coffee earlier.

'It's crazy,' I mused aloud, looking at Sam's plate, 'that in a country where a large part of the population had never eaten pork for seven centuries, there is now such a large pork culture.'

Boldly, I took a slice of raw ham from her plate and sank

my teeth into it, ripping it to shreds and chewing hard. My jaws stiffened, and I needed all my energy to chew it away.

Sam eagerly cut into a shiny pitch-black sausage. 'In the past, at my grandmother's, we got red cabbage with apple and fried black pudding. My grandfather slaughtered the pig himself. I still see grandma stir around in that barrel of dark red blood, and we children played with the pig bladder.'

I groaned and sighed: 'If only I was a vegetarian.'

She laughed. 'That's crazy. I have no problem with meat at all.'

'I meant: how come so many people eat pork in an ex-Muslim country?'

'Maybe the Muslims started eating pork to hide their true faith, to show they were good Christians after all?' she replied.

'Would it be like that? I can't imagine it. In their eyes, pigs were unclean animals.' Absently, I poked the soggy omelet and chewed a part of it with long teeth.

'Is it that bad? Let me have a taste.' Sam reached across the table and stuck her fork into my egg. 'Mm, bit greasy, but tasty.'

I slid half of the egg on her plate next to the meat and watched her, amazed at how she greedily downed my tortilla. I cut myself another bite and gagged when I tried to swallow.

Suddenly she was talking about someone called Lucy.

'Lucy and her husband had been trying to have a baby with IVF for three years, and it didn't work. Now, they signed up to adopt a child, even twins.'

'Lucy?'

'You know her, my colleague.'

Absently, I stared out of the window, trying to catch sight of the funeral procession in the distance. A burp left my mouth and I tasted fat olive oil. Nauseous, I swallowed back the acid that had come with it.

'Honey, if it doesn't work for us, we can also consider IVF, right?' Sam said.

Across the highway, suddenly, a large and colorful caravan pulled into the valley. Horses and camels led the way, carrying richly carved chests studded with silver and gold rivets. Men and women in white tunics thronged among the lively dressed animals. They walked closely together along the winding road into the valley. It was an impressive procession, and I was amazed that I hadn't seen that road before.

'What doesn't work?' Alarmed, I suddenly understood what Sam suggested. '

A child!'

'Sam,' I sighed, focusing on her again. 'I don't want children! We've talked about that dozens of times.' I pushed the words out of my mouth.

'But Jacob, it would be wonderful and good for our relationship. I'm thirty-eight, you're forty-five; my biological clock is ticking. You also agreed, I remove the IUD.'

Did Morayma and Boabdil have children? I had no idea. But his mother was there in the caravan. His father, the old king, was already dead and buried years before on the mountain peak, the Mulhacén.

'No, Squirrel, I didn't agree. You, yourself decided to have it removed,' I said firmly. 'Again, in case I haven't been clear enough: I don't want to bring children into this world.' Saying the words wore me out.

'Jacob, that's such a cliché. Why can't you believe that our children contribute something positive to this world.'

'I doubt that. One day you will thank me for not having them.'

'When I'm old and lonely in a nursing home, no way,' said Sam. 'You also have children for your old age, you know.'

'Never! Look at my mother. We have nothing in common. Inez chased me away with her possessiveness, and now she's lonely.' I grudgingly pushed my plate away.

Since I was thirteen, Inez and I had been together. She clung to me, her only child, and steered my life dominantly in the direction she had in mind for me. As long as I lived at home, I didn't notice it; there was something pleasant about our symbiosis, and above all, easy. But when I lived independently, she called me every day, and her dependence oppressed me. After I was living with Sam, my relationship with Inez deteriorated. Sam thought I should free myself from her. So, I tried to see my mother less and less and never called her.

'Yeah, that's dumb and pathetic, poor Inez, but I would never treat my kids the way she treated you.'

'Precisely. And about that, I have my doubts,' I said.

'What a rotten comment. I love children, I will be a great mother.' Sam also pushed her plate away.

'Sorry, just kidding.'

'Damn, man, why does everything always has to be so difficult with you? Why don't you just want a child too?' She used her spoiled pouting voice.

That tone irritated me, but I held back. 'Well, what happens if you have a kid you don't like? A bad ass, a criminal, a drug addict, or an invalid?'

'Bastard.' Sam furiously untied her ponytail and twisted the rubber band around it again, her mouth drawn into a straight line.

We were almost there. A bit more, and she'd be silent for hours. The atmosphere would be ruined, so I said conciliatorily: 'We're already somewhat older, honey. My father was over fifty when I was born. I don't want to be a father, especially not an old father.'

'You are not yet fifty. But you're right, so we'd better start sooner than later.' She gulped down her wine, started to say something, but our dessert was put on the table. Our plates were taken away. Mine still half full.

'Coffee?' she asked briefly.

'Yes please, you?'

'No, I have to pee and go outside into the sun. Are you coming then?'

I breathed a sigh of relief. I saw her gesture to the waiter, and he brought me a cup of coffee. Freed from her presence, I sank into deep thought.

I had just witnessed, from a far distance, two parades. A silent vigil commemorating the dead, and a lively caravan on their way to exile. Both scenes had happened in my mind, confirming that the sage worked and was a hallucinogen.

Stirring my coffee, I suddenly found myself in jail again, two weeks after my twenty-first birthday in 1984. I became involved in some riot and had thrown a stone at a police officer and was arrested. The next day my father died, and I couldn't go to the funeral. I imagined the black-clad guests escorting my dad to his final resting place under the blinding sun on the French Riviera. I had never said a proper goodbye to him. I should have felt remorse about that, but it hardly bothered me; I had built a rough stone wall around my feelings.

Dad left Inez when I was thirteen. He had started a love affair with Rachel, our neighbor in Jerusalem. She had a house in Nice and they went to live there.

Before my parents split up, dad communicated with me through my mother: 'Your father tells you to comb your hair before you come to dinner.' Or, 'He asks how school is going.' Or, 'He wants to know who you played with today.' After their divorce, our conversations went through Rachel. Dad never asked me things directly.

The last time I said to Rachel, 'Tell him he's an asshole.' After that, we didn't speak for two years.

Shortly before his death, he called me. We were both speechless. My nerves raced through the empty phone line.

Then he said, 'Jacob? Boy, I just want to hear your voice.'

In the background, Rachel prompted him. What should I say? Participate in that sentimental nonsense? Pretending we had a great relationship? The fact that my father died while I was in prison was hard. I never took time to mourn his death. A wave of regret hit the wall after all. Stone after stone, disappointment upon disappointment, I erected that wall with my own hands. Ever since my childhood. No one could see over it. My father? Never again. My two half-brothers? Not. My mother? Would I ever allow her? Sam? Sometimes she would push a little against the wall, and sometimes, suddenly, she would stick a little finger into a joint that was a bit crumbly. Like today, when she noticed the resemblance between Inez and Boabdil's mother. She had picked a loose stone. Most of the time, she didn't notice that she was hurting me, and then she would end the conversation with something like: 'You had an unprocessed childhood.' Or, 'You've got a hell of a trauma there, Jacob. You should talk to a psychologist.'

I would quickly joke and re-cement the stone. But at this moment, I had the feeling that I was picking at the mortar myself and a stream of lava flowed from a crack.

A push on my shoulder woke me up. 'Hey man, I'm sitting outside, endlessly waiting for you. What are you doing? You look hazy. Come on, we have to go to Granada.'

I swallowed the lump in my throat and noticed that I was almost crying, for God's sake.

GRANADA

The flamenco bar

*I*n Granada, we found a simple hotel in the city center, between the Plaza de Trinidad and the Cathedral. Sam enjoyed the hustle and bustle of the city more than I did and she studied the menus of the many restaurants and tapa bars hanging next to the entrances. A guitar player strummed his guitar on a street corner. I silently absorbed the Arab atmosphere, the typical buildings with columns, arches and colorful tile tableaus.

That evening, we strolled through the Albacín, the Arab quarter, famous for its narrow winding alleys with hundreds of steps between countless squares. I was intrigued by the socalled 'Carmens', impressive houses behind high gates and surrounded by gardens with century-old trees.

Finally, we arrived at the Plaza San Nicolas. My heart jumped when I saw the Alhambra, mesmerizingly illuminated by dozens of floodlights. This colossal edifice dominated the entire city. To the left of those rough brown-red walls and towers lay the Sierra Nevada, a hulking, dark beast that watched over the Alhambra.

'There used to be eternal snow on those peaks,' I said to Sam. 'The Arabs sourced the meltwater to irrigate their gardens.'

'Why isn't there any snow now?' she asked.

Shrugging my shoulders, I thought of my illusion this

afternoon. I said: 'What do you think of global climate change?'

She didn't answer; she got distracted by a group of barking dogs, hanging around some hippies. With my back to the bustling crowd, I looked in awe at the fairy-tale fortress and let my imagination run wild, trying to see what it was like inside those rough enigmatic walls. Because of all the books I had devoured, I could see the Alhambra clearly in my imagination, as if I had been there hundreds of years ago. Or had I already been inside the Alhambra? In a former life?

Sam and I wandered back through the cosy, dimly lit alleys with lively bars everywhere. On a terrace, we sat down, and ordered two glasses of country wine and nibbled on nuts and olives. I watched the passers-by and saw in every Spaniard Moorish traits: dark hair, fiery eyes, sometimes a stocky build. The waiter served a plate with meatballs; I left them to Sam, who crammed them down, despite all the meat she had already eaten this afternoon. It was well after eleven, and I suggested we head to our hotel. I wanted to be fit tomorrow, but unsurprisingly, we got lost. We wandered through alleys, crossed squares, and went up and down.

'We are walking in circles,' I said.

'I don't care. I love it here. Listen!' She stopped, her index finger raised, her head slightly tilted. I heard a deep male voice lament, accompanied by rhythmic hand clapping and guitar music. I wanted to walk on, but Sam pulled me along. A few minutes later, we were standing in a bustling pub with a crowd of clapping onlookers, while gypsies performed a flamenco act. A haze of blue cigarette smoke hung in the austere room. Four men in white shirts, black trousers and hats, red chokers around their necks and red sashes around their hips were standing in a circle. Between them circled four young women, their hair twisted at the back of their heads and wearing flared green dresses with white dots. Heels clicking on the stone floor, hands clapping above their heads, and they twisted their hips bold and sultry.

'This is the real Andalusia. Jacob, this is so cool; I had hoped to see this,' Sam shouted in my ear.

I grinned at the sunburned head of a fellow tourist in Bermuda shorts and wondered if this theatre was staged every night for tourists. I decided to swallow my cynicism for the sake of my girlfriend, who watched the young women open-mouthed. They were belly dancing to the rhythm of the music, till one of the men came to the center, the women stood stock-still. The man, with an extra-wide satin sash around his hips, his hair billowing at the back of his neck, synched seamlessly with the music. I didn't know why, but he touched something inside me.

Sam and I met during a tango dance course. But after two lessons I'd given up. Although I loved the music, I didn't like the fixed dance pattern. I wanted to take my own steps. Sam, disappointed to see me go, invited me to a pub where the group went afterwards. She turned out to be a gang leader, and the pints of beer were hard to hold off. I kept in the background, occasionally making an amusing remark, which was especially appreciated by Sam.

How that first night in her company came to an end? I have no idea. But the next morning, we looked into each other's eyes. Hers were green with brown spots, which intrigued me enough to make her breakfast and answer her voicemail a few days later. And the following week, I was back in 'The Staggering Stag' waiting for the group. A week later, I moved in with her because I had to leave my rental rooms.

Sam, stamping and clapping, sang low from her throat: 'Ole, ole.' And the next moment, she stood among the dancers, tapping on her sandals as if she was wearing heavy heels. She made no sound, but her movements were right, and her dance was well received by the audience, who cheered and applauded. Everyone became infected by the elated mood. Sam pulled me onto the dance floor. Cautiously I moved my hips, pretending to perform a self invented belly dance. I clicked my tongue and clapped my hands over my head.

Overwhelmed by the same inability as during the tango lessons, I left the dance floor as soon as possible. Sweat poured down my back, and I was gasping as if I had just climbed a mountain. Those few steps had left me breathless because of the stuffy, oxygen-poor air, I said to myself. My side stung, and I tried to regulate my breathing with my fingers between my ribs. Slowly I started to feel better again.

The exciting dance was over; Sam left the floor and came to me. There was a moment of rest. The man in the red sash stood alone in the center of the floor, eyes closed, and arms crossed over his chest. He started to move to the rhythm of soft guitar strumming and began spinning, slowly, then faster and faster, to the rhythm of only his heels, the guitar, and the quiet clapping of the women. His arms swung out. He turned, and turned, and turned. When the music stopped the dancer froze; with his legs together, he balanced on the tips of his toes. His arms were stretched, like the wings of a bird, as if he flew somewhere between heaven and earth.

Dead silence dominated the room, till deep and low, from somewhere in his diaphragm, he began to emit heart-rending sounds as if he wanted to express an intense sadness.

I felt goosebumps on my arms and didn't know what happened to me. The movement, the music, my own breathing, everything seemed perfectly coordinated, and that confused me. I saw an apparition in that veiled light of the smoky room as if something divine held me captive. Through the man, his emotion, and my sensitivity, I looked into the darkness of my mind. I saw something I didn't recognize, didn't even know existed. And it flew away again, carried by the sound of the music.

The somber mood changed; people were happy again. The dancer beckoned Sam with three fingers of his open hand and a smile on his lips. Shyly she stepped to the center, he bowed and then stepped aside. Sam stood alone with the sound of strumming guitars. She started to move calmly, completely involved in her feelings, with closed eyes. She danced to the beat of the music, faster and faster, her hair whirling around her head.

Pride swept through me, as I clapped at the rhythm. This was my girlfriend!

Soon the dance floor filled again with exuberant dancers. I withdrew and wriggled my way through the crowd to the bar, and ordered a beer.

That feeling from before haunted me. The wall inside me had been hit and crumbled. Hadn't I always managed to stop that feeling? I didn't want to feel melancholy, sadness, guilt, pain, all those big words Sam used so easily.

I closed my eyes and was back in that long hallway, a

cavern with no windows, just doors. Closed doors. How could I know which door I had to go through? Woe with me if I stepped into the wrong room. So, I waited for someone. Someone, who would open a door and push me into my dormitory, where I was the victim of thirty staring faces. Boys in uniforms between eight and thirteen. They knew their way around in the boarding school perfectly, and I still had no clue. Why was I so lost?

With my eyes down, I strolled through the long rows of beds with grey blankets. To the left of each headboard was a grey metal locker. The boys snickered behind my back. Then, somewhere halfway through, an empty bed seemed to be mine; I didn't recognize it from the other nights.

Upset, I longed for my own room at home, where Inez's homemade butterfly mobiles hung from the ceiling. Colored crepe paper lights lit my room and the yellow and red walls I had painted myself.

That first year, alone at the international school in Milan, I went through a baptism by fire, and I couldn't cope. I was scared and home sick. I visualized myself in that lonely bed again. On the left a row of boys under grey blankets, on the right a row of boys under grey blankets and opposite me, only beds with boys under grey blankets. I was as grey as all the other ones. Nobody saw me.

That grey feeling of my youth overwhelmed me in this Spanish bar. Poor soul, I told myself. I pulled a silly clown face at a man next to me. He rolled a cigarette and offered me his tobacco sack. I rolled one and inhaled the smoke deep into my lungs. I was a pathetic weak ass; I definitely failed Sam. She needed a frivolous guy who would laugh and dance with her. A cheerful bloke. Not a boring yo-yo like me. I still remember the fiasco of our first carnival together. That wasn't for me at all. I saw myself acting crazy and felt embarrassed. We were too different. But someone like Sam is good for me; she keeps me focused, and is more sociable than I am. She is a bit like Inez, who also arranged everything for me. I hated that, but let it happen out of convenience.

Exhausted, I drifted along to the rhythm of the music. The smoky room and the few cigarette puffs tightened my brain, and I felt nauseated. Just in time, Sam put her arms around me and pressed her sweaty body against mine.

'It's already past two; shall we go?' I yawned unabashedly.

'I could dance for hours, Prick. But you're right. Let's go.'

We walked out of the alley, following another couple, and stood within two minutes on the Plaza de Trinidad, almost next to our hotel.

I fell on the bed; Sam took a shower. Afterwards, she snuggled euphorically against me.

'Why do you love me?' I asked. That was asking for trouble.

'Because you love me too.' She began to kiss me sensually.

Was that all? That easy? Fortunately, she didn't push for sex; she was already half asleep. Before I fell asleep too, I gently ran my index finger along her temple and thought I love her spontaneity. Then, I saw the dancing man again and the divinity of his movements. He had been the trigger for my mood. He was in touch with his feelings, stood in the present, but moved between present and past. Strange that I was suddenly open to such a vague concept. Perhaps it was the sage... ? But I didn't finish the thought.

The Alhambra

The next morning there was a long line at the cash register near the main entrance of the Alhambra. We were in back of the line but it soon became apparent that we were in the wrong queue. With our reservation ticket, we could go straight through, and a little later, we joined the hordes. Japanese, English, German and Dutch tourists all wanted to be part of this mega complex's beating heart. We shuffled along the foundations of the buildings; people once lived and worked here. Roses bloomed in the gardens. Fresh water rippled through an ancient water gutter along the path to the Moorish bathhouse.

While I looked around, Sam disappeared into a souvenir shop. Besides Moorish trinkets, postcards, and numerous plaster friezes with Arabic characters, they also sold colorful glazed tiles, the so-called azulejos. I didn't like souvenirs, but followed her inside and found almost immediately what I was looking for: a box of walnut wood, the size of a large matchbox and the lid was engraved with Arabic characters. I paid quickly without Sam noticing and left the shop. Leaning against a wall, waiting for Sam, I read in my booklet that Alhambra means: 'the red'. The palace was built by Arab dynasties on the foundations of a mainly Jewish city at the end of the eleventh century.

Again, I had that feeling of a déja-vu, just like yesterday afternoon on the Plaza de San Nicolas. Or were these the hallucinations fueling my latest obsession?

Sam walked out of the shop with a plastic bag on her wrist.

'Nice for Mom.' She proudly showed me a kitschy tile.

I ignored her and said: 'We have to be at the palace in ten minutes.'

'So, we're in no hurry.'

'Please. I don't want to be late.'

'Sure.' Sam rolled her eyes and pulled her hair back into a ponytail.

'The ancient Islamic world consisted of several Caliphates. The Umayyads were a royal family in Syria from Damascus.' I told her what I just read while we walked onwards. 'The Abbasids reigned in Persia, nowadays Iraq and Iran, with Baghdad as its capital.'

'Cut the crap, Jacob; let's buy some water.' Sam stopped at an ice cream stall.

I waited till she had paid, and then I carried on: 'The Abbasids defeated the Umayads, but a young prince, Abd-al Rahman I, survived the massacre. He left Damascus with some followers, went to the west, and ended up in the south of Spain. He built Cordoba in Al Andalus, around 750.'

'Anda luz, would that actually mean, 'walking light'?' Sam mused.

'Nice idea, but I read somewhere that it comes from the Vandals, the Germans who'd settled here in the 5th century, and called the country Vandalusia.'

'I like 'walking light,' she muttered. 'So, those Arabs came and stayed in power for seven centuries. They brought wealth, education and became famous.'

'Yes. Until, say, the twelfth century Muslims, Jews and Christians co-existed fairly peacefully. They tolerated each other's rituals and customs and exchanged norms and values.'

'What a pity it couldn't stay that way; sooner or later, there will always be animosity,' Sam sighed. 'And the Alhambra, where does this building appear in this story?'

'The Alhambra was a Jewish fortress. It wasn't until after the eleventh century that various sultans of the Nasrid dynasty extended it. One sultan built the Princess Palace called The Generalife. Another planted the gardens. And another sultan built the Alcazaba over there.' I pointed to the colossal square tower, which towered over the complex, overlooking Granada's Vega. 'We're going there later. Look, on this map you see the military quarters and the souks, a kind of medina with squares where they held markets. Actually, this whole complex was a city.'

'But why is it so special? It's even called the eighth world wonder.'

'The Arabs were masters of sophisticated architecture. They understood the art of decorating like no other people. The Alhambra has survived the past five centuries despite considerable destruction and incorrect restorations. Yet, this is Europe's most important Islamic building!'

'And what is this monstrous creature?' Sam walked through an immense gate into the open arena of the square building we had passed.

'The palace of Charles V. He was the son of Philip the Handsome and Joanna the Mad. Her parents were Ferdinand and Isabella, the famous Catholic royal couple. Charles started building this palace in 1525 and demolished a part of the Nasrid palace to make space for this colossus.'

'I think it's a monster.'

'Me too. Yet, I read that this building is the most important Renaissance building outside Italy.' I grabbed Sam by the arm. 'Come on, it's past twelve.'

Around the corner, dozens of people stood in the partial shade, waiting to enter the Nasrid Palace. The wooden door, which hung heavily in its brass hinges, was just opening. Through a narrow corridor, over a worn floor and along colorful wall tiles the tourists were led into the first room: the Mexuar.

In awe, I shuffled around, not knowing where to look first. I tried to ignore the buzz of people around me. The Arabic characters in the off-white stucco caught my attention. Poems and texts from the Quran. The motto 'Nothing but Allah's Victory' appeared a few times in every room. But also, one of the most famous surahs from the Quran: 'Besmellah rahmane rahim': In the name of Allah. He is sweet. He gives. He forgives.

Sam looked at all the beautiful artefacts through the display of her digital camera. She walked ahead of me into the next room, and I lost sight of her. Somewhere, I would run into her again. That was nice about our relationship; in situations like this, she let me do my own thing, so we could share our experiences later to be surprised, how she had paid attention to totally different things than I had.

If only I were back in those days. Maybe I would see Morayma walking around, or Boabdil coming home from a battle and retiring with her to their private quarters. These halls were bare, without furniture, no colorful carpets lying on the ground or hanging on the walls. I leafed through Robert Irwin's book, 'The Alhambra', which had all kinds of interesting information one doesn't read in travel guides.

'The windows were so low because people mainly sat on carpets.' He wrote and suggested: 'Try to sit on the floor to have a taste of the view in those days.'

I found a quiet corner and followed his advice. Sitting cross-legged, my backpack in front of me, I looked out over the city of Granada. Indeed, this was different.

Suddenly, the tip of a shoe stung my side; someone almost tripped over me. Angry faces from visitors looked down on me. I mumbled some apologies and got up.

I crossed all the halls, then walked back to the Comares tower behind the court of the Myrtles. I would love to have a look back in time, smell the scents, see the colors. My hand reached for the matchbox and the new wooden box. I could transfer the paste here and throw the old matchbox away. The thought was mouth-watering, but I didn't dare to do it. There were too many people around me. Besides, it would be more practical to explore the Alhambra first.

I waited patiently for a group of Russians to saunter after their guide into the next room. I took a breath and let the simplicity of the long pond in the court of the Myrtles sink in. I read in the booklet: 'Today the pond is bordered by myrtle hedges, but there used to be orange trees, casting their shadows in the water. This is the perfect space, in width and length.' Indeed, the proportions felt right. Only now, I saw the corner of the monstrous palace of Charles V slide, barbarously, and without any compassion, into the refined Palace of the Nasrids.

The room filled with new tourists, while I stood in a corner to reading the book. Moments later, I felt a familiar chin on my shoulder. 'Come on, Prick, we have to move on; there's so much more to see.'

'Charles V built that monster but never visited it himself,' I told her, closing the book. Angered by this barbarity, I followed Sam into the Patio de los Leones. A small courtyard, surrounded by a gallery supported by round, slender columns, where in the center stood the famous fountain with its lions.

'It has been copied and photographed at least a thousand times.'

'Jacob, I don't understand why these figures are animals. Earlier, you said that Islam forbade to display images of animals or humans. Only decorations with geometric shapes were allowed.'

'Yes, good point. Perhaps the lions were placed around it later. Let's see what Irwin says about it.' I flipped through the book and read aloud: 'The lions are from the fourteenth century and were sculpted after an example of a few centuries older Jewish fountain. Because the lions are so stylized, they were not considered animal figures.'

Next to the lion patio was the hall of the Abencerrajes. The Abencerrajes were powerful advisers of the Nasrid kings. During Boabdil's reign, they were slaughtered here in cold blood by their adversaries: the followers of the old king, Boabdil's father. The blood could still be seen on the walls, I read in Irwin's book, but he also wrote that all these stories were based on legends.

Sighing, I closed the book and put it in my backpack. My little finger rubbed against the boxes now sitting brotherly in the side compartment. Would the paste show me what really had happened? If I took the Sage of the Ghost's now, would

I experience the truth? Or was I a victim of fantasies fueled by my own hallucinations?

My gaze wandered through the crowds. I recognized Sam by her chamois leather backpack, her avocado green T-shirt, and the back of her head with the ponytail. She took a picture of two laughing Japanese girls standing in front of the lion fountain.

Together we roamed further through the rooms and entered the apartment of the American diplomat and writer, Washington Irving. He rented rooms here around 1829.

'Here, he wrote his famous *Tales of the Alhambra,* I said to Sam, who stood before an open arched window and stared into the air-polluted fog that hung over the city of Granada. To our right the maze of the Albaicín, with green clusters of trees in the Carmens, was visible. To the left, the cathedral soared above the city center. From there, roads led out of the city. Colored dots of cars drove off and on. Behind the outer ring, construction cranes towered like herons on high legs between new residential areas to be built.

Washington wrote about the Arabs in Granada. How did that man research all those stories? I sat down on the floor again, leaning against the wall with closed eyes, trying not to hear the buzz around me. But Sam gave me no time and pulled me up. I was not allowed to take time and taste the atmosphere. We strolled further out into the gardens. The gardens are unique, Irwin wrote in his book.

Everywhere water rippled through gutters from pond to pond at different levels. Birds whistled. Sun and shade played a game with the leaves on the trees around us. This was an oasis. The sudden silence and tranquility, after the constant energy of people, were soothing.

'Let's stay here, Squirrel,' I said. 'This is heavenly peaceful. I want to read and write in my diary, muse a little. This is a place where special things have happened; I can feel it.'

'What's happening to you, Jacob? You sound so spiritual.' Sam smiled at me as if she liked my musings.

'Be patient with me, Sam; I'm figuring something out, something about myself.'

'Honey, it's about four o'clock. I'm hungry and thirsty, we were inside for hours. Didn't you promise me lunch at the Parador?'

I had hardly eaten the last three days; indeed, I felt a little hungry too. 'Okay, let's go and grab a bite at the Parador.'

Via a sturdy revolving gate, we left the gardens and passed a church that used to be a mosque, I'd read in Irwin's book. We arrived at the large public square, with shops and taxi's. I noticed not one attendant checked tickets at this exit.

The Parador

We walked to a Moorish building where the famous hotel, El Parador de San Francisco, was housed.

'Do you know why these chic hotels are called Parador?' Sam liked to show her knowledge through a question.

'You would say it has something to do with stopping. Parar means to stop, doesn't it?'

'Precisely. They were state hotels, always located in beautiful places and in stunning old buildings, like monasteries or castles. Chic but formal.'

'I think this Parador is a popular one and very expensive,' I said. 'A room costs at least five hundred euros a night. The building belonged to the former mosque; later, it became a Franciscan monastery.'

We peeked into the lounge, decorated in Arabic and Christian style with classical furniture, portraits, and engravings. Everywhere hung embroideries. The restaurant had a large terrace in a courtyard, dotted with tables and chairs. Only a few were occupied.

'There are thousands of tourists, and nobody has lunch here?' Sam looked around in surprise.

'Be happy; now we have private attention.'

We ordered water and a bottle of wine from the Rioja region. Sam looked at the menu as if her life depended on food. Maybe it did, I thought; sometimes, a meal seemed the only thing that interested her.

'Leg of lamb with prunes, stew with rabbit, sea bream. And the specialties: gazpacho Andalus, tortilla de Sacromonte. Do you feel like having an omelet again, or do you want Pollo a la Alpujarrena? I think that's chicken with a lot of garlic. Oh, and I'm going for dessert: Piononos de Santa Fe; I've read about that.' Sam licked her lips with glittering eyes.

'I don't need much; a salad will do.'

'Great, let's have a salad first. I'll take the chicken, you the leg of lamb?'

I nodded absently. I was in a weak mood and allowed myself to be patronized, to keep the relationship lovingly.

A stylish waiter brought a basket of bread and a bowl of

olives. He opened the bottle of wine at our table and poured a little into Sam's glass with one hand behind his back. She tasted and nodded approvingly.

When the man was gone, I asked: 'So, how did you like the palace?'

'Beautiful. Those tiles, I think I took at least eighty pictures.' She pulled out her camera and showed me how to scroll through the photos. The light was too bright, and I could see myself reflected in the display.

'What about you?' she asked, munching on a piece of bread.

'Fascinating. I would like to walk around here for days, there is so much to see. As I said earlier in the garden, all my senses are stimulated. I felt so alive.' I placed the knife and fork straight next to my plate, looked up again and said hesitantly: 'In my soul, I hear the footsteps and whisperings of those days. I would like to go all the way back in time. Meeting people, hearing their voices, smelling their scents, even wearing their clothes.'

'Do you want to convert to Islam?' Sam laughed heartily as if it was a good joke, she even laid her hand forgivably on mine.

I grinned a sort of reply. Secretly a plan had formed in my head, I would go back and have some sage. But when? That was the big question. Unfortunately, I could not discuss any of this with her. She wasn't open to experiments. When I was sixteen, I smoked my first joint with a friend; it was awesome! Later, we tried other mind-altering drugs, magic mushrooms, and LSD. I never had any regrets. On the contrary, I remember those experiences as the most beautiful journeys of my life. In William Burroughs' *Junkie,* I read what drugs and narcotics do to you. Via Carlos Castaneda, who was experimenting with peyote, I understood I had to be careful. When I told Sam about these experiences, she thought it was creepy and dangerous.

The salad was served. I picked an olive, half a tomato and a piece of tuna and felt already satisfied. And yet, I mused further, I was not completely involved then. It was not close to the experience in the hallucinatory inn when I met the Moor. What had Angel said again? 'My herbal paste is not toxic, but the experience is addictive.' Yes, I was willing to believe that. I started to long for a new trip.

Sam ate more of the salad than I did. 'I really want that chicken,' she chatted. 'Be careful that you don't starve of hunger, you hardly ate the past few days. Ah, here it comes.'

My lamb came in a tagine. With the napkin ready, Sam took the chimney-shaped lid off my plate. She poked her fork in the meat and devoured a mouthful. 'Aw, shit. Glowing hot.'

'Own fault, dear, you're too greedy.'

Guilty of her gluttony, she watched as I cautiously began to chew my meat, which was butter soft. 'Nice,' I said. 'Don't worry, I'll leave something for you.'

Her chicken came too, and instantly, she turned her lurking, mouth-watering gaze to her own plate.

'This is something else.' Sam licked her fingers. 'So far we had menu del día, that peasant Alpujarra dish is pretty greasy.'

After more than two hours of slowly feasting on the food, I left half of the tajine with lamb for her. We were the only guests left and I asked for the bill. Sam snatched the gold-edged leather folder off me.

'It was my treat to you,' I said weakly.

Sam studied the bill with raised eyebrows and counted the total amount several times.

'I wouldn't do that, Prick. These kinds of extravagances come out of our household purse.' With a poker face, she placed three fifty notes in the leather pouch.

'Well,' I said, as we walked away towards the exit, 'now I understand why we were almost the only guests.'

Sam nodded: 'A ten-euro menu is crude and rustic but a lot cheaper.'

'We haven't even been to the Generalife.' Disappointed, I looked at the sign, pointing the way to the Princess Palace.

'What is that, General life?' She emphasized the name in English.

'Generalife,' I said. 'Rhymes on thief. I would love to go there. The vegetable and flower gardens are divided by hedges and walls, and there are ponds with fountains everywhere. Everything has been restored here in recent years.'

'But what is it?'

'The gardens of the Generalife are famous, and the Palace at the far end was the weekend retreat of the Nasrids, while the Alhambra had been their hunting lodge.'

'Jacob, I'm so full. I need to lay down first.'

'What a culture barbarian you are,' I teased her.

'I should have known better than falling in love with a history teacher.' She laughed coquettishly.

'Yes, a cook would have been more helpful.'

'Sorry, I've always had that before my ovulation, craving sweets and good food.'

'Luckily, you don't have a tendency to get fat.'

She enjoyed these kinds of conversations, it was about her, and I showed my involvement. The true relationship, she thought. But I felt poor and barren. It reminded me of Inez's endless chitchat. As a teenager, I had no excuse for that and said yes or no. I'd rather talk about essential things, but I didn't know how to do that at the time. And maybe, I still have no idea about the essence of things.

When we left the Alhambra through the main entrance, I saw a bookshop. If I wasn't allowed to go to the Generalife, a brief browse through those books, had to be permitted.

Sam shrugged. 'Okay, then. I'll wait in the shade. Just got a message from mum.' Across the road, she found an empty bench in the shade.

Eagerly, I searched through the piles of books. Books about the history of Al Andalus, the Moors, and the Alhambra. They were mostly Spanish-language copies, but there were also books in English. I kept putting books next to the cash register. Washington Irving's *Tales of the Alhambra* and his *The Conquest of Granada, Leo Africanus* by Amin Maalouf, and a Spanish version of *Granada* by Radwa Ashoer. I found a book about Boabdil and his family, and finally, I paid with my credit card.

Back into the bright light, I saw Sam excitedly talking to two gypsy women in colorful skirts, firm bosoms, and thick black hair. We'd noticed them before when they forcefully waved rosemary sprigs in front of tourists. As soon as Sam saw me, she left the women and came to me. 'Are those bitches crazy? First, they start a sweet chat. Then, one took my hand, started stroking her finger along my lifeline and said: 'Muchos niños, niñas tambien.'

'Cuando?' When?, I asked.

'Próximo año. Gemelos,' she said. Mind you, twins! Then she wanted money. I pushed a euro into her hand, but that was not enough.

'Cinco,' she said, five.

I said no, and she squeezed my arm hard.' With a painful grin, she showed me her bruises. A little further on, the women attacked yet another victim.

On the bus to the city, Sam saw my heavy bag. 'Books? Prick, aren't you exaggerating a little?'

'What do you mean?'

'Are they about that sultan of yours?'

'Some of them are, and his wife, Morayma. That couple fascinates me.'

'And what's so fascinating about that couple?'

'Nothing really, I don't know, or yes, I do. She was his only wife, which is unusual for a Muslim, and his attempts at reconciliation with the Christians came to nothing. It's a bit like today. Islam against the rest of the world.'

'But you also once said he was not much more than a puppet on a string?'

'I know. There are so many stories and legends about that time. Nobody really knows what happened. I want to read all those books and draw my own conclusions.'

'You want to know my opinion? Books are bullshit. Why not just enjoy the experience of today. All those facts, let them be. All those scientific words and stuff... I don't want to know. I prefer to listen to my feelings in the present.'

'You are right, I want that too, but I also need books. I'm a history nerd, you know that.'

'Of course, but I'm in contact with myself; you are not.'

'What do you mean?'

'You are too intellectual, and you have a huge ego. You consider yourself important and are far from being in essential contact with yourself. Miles away.'

'Is that so?' I said calmly. 'You say you know me? but I don't recognize myself in your words at all.'

'Okay, Mr. deaf ears.' She cut me off bluntly and said in another voice: 'It's almost five-thirty; what are we going to do?'

I would prefer to sit on a shady terrace with my books, but I kept that to myself.

'Let us drop your book load in the hotel, have a brief nap, and we'll go back into town,' Sam suggested enthusiastically. 'The shops stay open till nine.'

History lessons

Somehow, I didn't fall asleep, and by three o'clock I crawled out of bed, wide awake. I slid the only chair in the room over to the open window. Once seated, I pulled the books out of the bag and read the titles and blurbs thoroughly by the yellowish light of the lamppost in the street.

Outside, the buzz of the city drifted along, balmy breezes of the summer night blew in. Somewhere there was the whimper of a tomcat, like a crying baby. Some youngsters stood under my window, babbling and laughing. Then they left and it became quiet.

I used to study historical facts and read quickly. Most of the stories were based on legends; I knew that already and also why. The main reason was Cardinal Cisneros. In 1499 he decreed a major book burning in Granada and the Christians destroyed many, if not all, Arabic writings. A method great rulers enforced or utilized; by erasing the past, they made their own reign more important. Last year, I gave a lesson about this issue in the pre-university classes. In 213 BC, the Chinese emperor Shih Huang Ti had burned all documents of his predecessors, so the new age would start with him. He even had teachers incinerated who taught old ideas. Over the centuries, books and manuscripts have always been destroyed. To me, as a historian, this short-sighted arrogance was unacceptable. But I also knew it would not end with the last book burning, Kristallnacht, in Nazi Germany.

I read about January 2nd 1492, when the last Caliph Muhammad I, surnamed Boabdil, officially handed the keys of the Alhambra over to Los Reyes Catholicos, the Catholic Monarchs. I read about Columbus, who sailed out on *The Santa Maria* later that year to discover new land. He was financed by those same kings. I also read new information, like facts and details of the Reconquista, that had eluded me during my studies. All those stories about battlefields and wars over centuries, what's new after all, could be skipped. What I liked was the psychology behind events. The people and their reasons. At the moment, my main subject was only one man: the last sultan of Granada, the Spanish peasant I had met in Angel's inn. I had a strong feeling I had known him in a previous life, I felt connected to him.

I read somewhere that Boabdil was a power-hungry man, who, to save his own skin, opposed his father and handed him over to Ferdinand. In another story, he was portrayed as a gentle man, not a fighter, but a coward. And yet another historian claimed he had no choice. It simply was the fate of the Caliphate of Granada to be handed over to the Christians sooner or later. The countless feuds and quarrels between the ruling families severely undermined the authority and prestige of the Islamic power. They caused their own demise, and Boabdil had fallen victim to it. That's how I saw it too; as if my own brother had failed, and I felt sorry for him.

I read about Boabdil's father, Muhammad X, Muley Hacen, the ruling sultan in Granada between 1470 and 1480. I envisioned a stern and unjust man, who instead feasted and amused himself while his Caliphate crumbled. He imprisoned his wife and son and refused to honor the tax treaty with the Catholics. His reign marked the definitive beginning of the end.

Suddenly, I was brought back to my youth. On my father's desk were a pile of tax-blue envelopes. It must have been shortly before my parents' divorce. Pa sat in his study, resting his head in his hands. Apparently, he was in big trouble. A month or two later, my mother and I lived in an apartment in Hackney. One day, I came home from school. I stopped on the stairs because I heard my mother's voice on the phone. Emphatic and resentful.

'I demand that you check where he goes.'

'No, sir, it's not right what my ex-husband has been up to.'

-

'Why am I reporting him? Because he told me to leave.'

-

'Yes, that's how we treat each other. By the way, that's none of your business. I'm just giving you a tip. Look into his bank account in Zurich, Switzerland.'

-

'Exactly, sir. Goodbye, sir, and have a nice day.'

That was Inez, rock hard. But so was dad; he had literally kicked us out without a penny. She was so angry and wanted revenge. I've always suspected she later had some regrets about that phone call. In any case, her move marked the end of my father's career as a consul.

I blinked away the memory, let bygones be bygones. I wanted to read about Boabdil and his father.

King Ferdinand was outraged at Muley Hacen's lack of cooperation and attacked the fortified city of Alhama de Granada in 1482. After this first successful victory, Ferdinand got a taste for it. In the next ten years, many more of such fierce skirmishes between Christians and Arabs would visibly crumble the Caliphate of Granada. Ferdinand's famous words at that time were: 'Granada is slowly falling apart, the way a pomegranate loses its seeds one by one.' The memory of my father, who bubbled up among the facts of more than five hundred years of history, distracted me.

After the divorce and his early retirement, he lived in Nice with Rachel, his third wife. She was my father's age and had been the best friend of dad's first wife, Hannah, who died in a car accident. We didn't get alimony, and Inez didn't want it either, so we lived off assistance until she started earning money by giving drama lessons and some weaving and knitting work. A few years later, it turned out that the flat we were renting was in my name. Without our knowledge, dad had arranged that the rent Inez paid him, came back to me.

'You were born out of love, son,' Inez used to say, but I had my doubts about that. I was conceived inadvertently. Inez was the au pair for my two older half-brothers, Peter and William, and she had easily found her way to the lonely, grieving widower's bed. When she was later side-lined, she said with a twisted face: 'Hannah was his great love. I was just the band-aid on the wound.'

That's how I felt too. The band-aid on the wound. When dad looked at my half-brothers, his eyes lit up. When he looked at me, his face darkened. He always saw my mother in me, and after the divorce, he didn't want anything to do with her, nor me. I thought.

I shut my eyes to search for some good memories, but I couldn't think of any. I picked up the book again and read: Muley Hacen died in 1485, his body was buried at the top of the highest mountain of the Iberian Peninsula, that mountain got his name.

The day before yesterday, I had literally seen his funeral; a procession of seemingly black ants meandering through the snow. At the time of his father's interment, Boabdil was imprisoned because of the battle of Lucena, and therefore not present at his father's funeral. Just like me. My father died exactly five hundred years after Boabdil's father in 1985, and I was in prison as well.

A month before my twenty-first birthday, my father called me. 'Jacob,' he said. 'Why don't you come to Nice. I'll pay for your trip. I need to talk to you. I want to tell you about my life, and I want to hear about yours.'

'I have exams, dad. I must study hard. I'll come in the summer holidays.' I didn't open one study book at that time. There had been actions against Thatcher, I was involved in. When my dad was dying, I made banners and bombs. Two weeks after my birthday, in late January, my father died of cancer. Dad wanted contact, he wanted to say goodbye, and I had ignored him. The day before his funeral, I was arrested. I did not think about him and had thrown my emotions behind the thick wall inside me. At the time, I was unaware of this. But now, writing these things down, I know it was like that. My mind drifted between then and now; I felt like I was gliding on two tracks, only five hundred years apart.

I tried to imagine Aisha, Muley Hacen's first wife and Boabdil's mother. He was her eldest son, her crown prince, the apple of her eye. Her face: a sharp nose, deep-set dark eyes, and her white hair tinted with henna, just like her hands and feet were covered with henna patterns. She ruled the harem and argued if she didn't get her way. With a surly face, which definitely didn't make her more beautiful, she looked at the younger, pretty women who were called to the old king's bed. Whatever ruse she devised, having her face painted like a young beauty, dressing in the most beautiful silk robes, the old king no longer chose her. He knew her tricks and grinned to himself. He was old, but not crazy. He saw through her schemes perfectly and had enough of her and that son of theirs, whom she propelled to the throne.

Muley Hacen's life changed completely during a battle near the ancient Roman provincial town of Guadix. An area with sand columns and craggy cliffs in a reddish color, and here and there a silhouette of an old tree cut out against the blue sky. The old king and his men headed home after the battle. Along the road, the foreman saw two eyes gleaming in a pile of rags and stopped.

'Christian Hound, rise up and salute your king,' he commanded sternly.

'Sire.' A young woman struggled to her feet and pleaded with the sultan, who rode next to the foreman. 'I am a Christian woman; my name is Isabelle de Solis. Por favor, I will do whatever you wish, but please, do not kill me.'

'Catch her. Take her to the palace,' was the King's short reply. They galloped back to Granada. The woman was send to the harem and washed and dressed in Arabic clothes. She was taken to the sultan, and for the second time that day, the old man succumbed to the light in her eyes.

'I'll call you Zoraya, and you'll marry me.'

Aisha also saw the light in the woman's eyes and knew instinctively, her time as the sultana had ended. This young woman had found the way to her husband's heart. She became his chosen one. Zoraya quickly dethroned Aisha, gained a lot of influence over Muley Hacen and gave him two more sons.

I compared the jealousy Aisha must have felt with my mother as she saw dad move more and more toward Rachel. Rachel was older, uglier, less whimsical, and less interesting than Inez, but she was solid, straightforward, and apparently made dad happy. Inez couldn't do that anymore.

'How is she, what is she doing?' mum asked, eyes bulging with jealous curiosity, as I told her about my holiday in Nice.

'She takes care of him, makes his sandwich, pours his drink and peels his orange because he doesn't want dirty fingers.'

'Looks like he lives with his housekeeper,' Inez sneered. 'What does he see in that ugly witch?'

'She's a treasure.' I defended Rachel because my father's third wife did those things also for me.

For a while, I gazed thoughtfully at the gnats swarming in the light of the street lantern. Where in the world would my brothers Peter and William hang out? After my parents' divorce, I probably met them three more times. They were both married; Peter had entered diplomatic service, just like dad and the last time I heard from William, he was in Australia.

Behind me, Sam turned around in bed and let out a snoring sigh. We hadn't made plans for tomorrow yet, but I was determined. I would go back to the Alhambra.

A few garbage collectors dumped the full containers from the restaurant next to the hotel into the smelly back of a garbage truck. The rotten smell almost made me gag. My eyes burned from staring in the dim light. Despite the muggy temperature, I shivered and went back to bed. I clung to Sam's warm body, and before I fell asleep, I saw on her neon-lit wristwatch that it was five-thirty.

Her noisy yawns and the patter of bare feet on the stone floor woke me up a few hours later. Sam disappeared into the bathroom, and I fell into a slumber again. Minutes later, she abruptly pulled the sheet from my naked body.

'Get out, you lazy bum.' She jumped on me and began to caress me in a way that usually worked, but today I kept my distance. She was undoubtedly fertile, and I wanted to go to the Alhambra. I pushed her away and dragged myself into the shower. Only when I turned the tap on cold, the sleep poured off my tired body, into the drain. While I shaved, Sam chatted incessantly at me from the bedroom.

'What are you up to?' I asked when I saw her heels and make-up.

'We're going to have a nice time in the city; I'm really looking forward to that. Last night, I saw a few shops with the latest fashion. Then we'll have lunch, and maybe there's still time to go to Lorca's birthplace or visit some art gallery.'

I'm not going into town. I don't feel like shopping at all.'

'Then, what do you want?'

'I would love to go back to the Alhambra.' The timid tone in my voice made me vulnerable and Sam strong. Sucker, why didn't I insist I had to go back. For several hours!

'Again? Wasn't yesterday enough?'

'I told you; I could have walked around there for days. At home we also do separate things. I never go shopping with you.'

'Okay, I'll go alone and enjoy myself, and you go to that old heap.'

Relieved the negotiation went fairly smoothly, I swallowed my indignation about 'that old heap'.

'Shall we meet for lunch at three o'clock?' she asked.

'Three o'clock?' I turned her wrist towards me and saw it was nearly nine-thirty. More than five hours, that had to work.

'Okay, three o'clock.'

We argued about where we would meet, and then I grabbed my backpack, put a book in it and was almost out of the room and down the stairs.

'Hey, Prick, why the rush? We're having breakfast first.'

'Oh yes, breakfast,' I muttered.

In a pub around the corner, a couple of men sat at the bar, sipping their coffee, and engrossed in the newspaper.

I ordered two cafe solo.

Sam asked for a tostada with olive oil and grated tomato. She gave me half, and that was more than enough. I waited impatiently for her to finish, so we could pay. But she was in no hurry and nibbled at her tostada, asking: 'Why did you ask me that anyway?'

'What?'

'The other night, after the flamenco evening. We were in bed, and you asked me why I love you.'

'Oh, that? You were dancing so great, and I felt like a boring pig. Not good enough for you.'

'Ah, nonsense.' She put her hand on my neck, caressingly plucked at the short hairs. 'But you do love me, don't you? I sometimes doubt it, you know, especially lately.'

'You really don't have to, but why are you bringing this up. At this moment?'

'Yesterday I kept forgetting, and this morning I wanted to make love, and once again you clearly didn't want to. So, I thought, I'd just ask what's the matter.'

'Don't worry, I'm not feeling too well.'

'How come?'

'I don't know; something is bothering me. My youth? Guilt?' The words came from a subconscious drawer, and perhaps there was some truth in them.

For a while, Sam looked at me thoughtfully, took a last sip

of coffee, and said: 'Thank you for telling me. When we get back, we'll visit Inez together. Would that help?'

'Mother? She has nothing to do with it,' I lied.

'Jacob, let's talk, please.'

I lightly kissed her mouth. 'Not now. See you at three.' I dashed off to the Plaza Nueva where I caught the bus to the Alhambra.

Mother and son

After ten o'clock, there was still a queue of visitors trying to obtain an admission ticket. I realised it was far too busy for my trip to the past. Stupid, I should have been here hours earlier, and how would I get in without a ticket? Via the outside avenue, I hurried along the complex through the Gate of Justice to the public square. Here were the toilet blocks, the souvenir shops and the taxi stand.

I stopped in front of the turnstile. Yesterday we had left the gardens via this gate. I looked around and, in the distance, saw an attendant talking to another guard. No visitors had left the gardens yet. Yesterday, I had seen a guard lifting the turnstile so it could turn freely in both directions. Heedless, I now did the same. I slid inside, lowered the gate back into its one-sided latch and disappeared into the silence among the green hedges. The scent of jasmine blossoms and roses fell over me like a freshly laundered sheet. Come to your senses, and prepare yourself, I mumbled. With the backpack on my knees, I sat down on a step and pulled the cord. Prepare myself? For what?

Acting faster than I could think, I had both boxes in my hand. I held my breath, and with a pounding heart, I flipped the paste over into the wooden box, amazed that their sizes were so equal. I took a reasonable piece, the size of my thumbnail, and put it under my tongue. With my eyes closed, I tasted a bitter flavor, which spread slowly into my mouth. It reminded me of the entrails of a poorly cleaned sardine. I opened my eyes and saw that nothing had happened. I longed for the Moor from the inn. I wanted to meet him again, but wondered if I would succeed during this reckless act. I had no idea if the sage would show me anything here at the Alhambra. Maybe nothing would happen at all. The small dose I had taken the day before yesterday also didn't yield anything. What did I expect actually? Why had Angel given me this crap? For the money? Was it really life-threatening? I must be crazy to believe in these things. A group of sparrows chirped and bathed happily in a shallow water gutter to the right of my feet; I looked at it absentmindedly. I wanted to observe but saw nothing. In the distance, a guard crossed the path. Luckily, he didn't notice me. Nobody expected anyone in the gardens yet. I got up and began to walk around hesitantly. Should I have taken more? Why didn't that stuff work? What should I do now? I was at the spot where we had left the palace yesterday. I entered the garden of Lindaraxa and walked back into the palace.

My ears strained to hear soft singing. Did I hear Arabic? The call to prayer? The light seemed to have changed. I turned and followed a man on leather babouches, dressed in a white tunic, with a bright, colorful turban on his head. He had passed me without seeing me. Yesterday it was empty here. Today there were colorful carpets on the floor, adorning the walls or hanging out of the windows with indigo, red, ochre, or green so intense as if a light shone behind them. I located the sonorous drone of prayer in the Albaicín on the other side of the river. Strong spicy scents of cinnamon and coriander drifted by. In the early morning light, I could see the mountains in the distance. Their tops were hidden under a white pleated cloth. Snow in August?

I followed the man, who carried a tray laden with fruit, he opened doors where there were walls yesterday. He set the tray down in front of a heavy wooden door, and took an immense key from his pocket, stuck it in the keyhole and turned it. As soon as he went in, I followed closely. The Comares Tower was the large square space behind the Patio de los Arrayanes. Yesterday, I had looked around here because, in this tower, the old king had locked up his wife and son.

I immediately saw what was going on. A younger version of the Moor from the inn sat on the tiled ledge along the wall. He was about fifteen or sixteen years old, and his black hair flowed over his shoulders. He had high cheekbones and fair skin, lighter than his mother. Aisha walked up and down the small space like a caged lioness, her mouth contorted into a sharp line. She stopped pacing, as the attendant stood in front of her with the tray in his hands. She moved the oranges, pomegranates, and nuts and pulled out some silk scarves.

'This is not enough. Rashid, get us more.'

The man put the tray down and disappeared. I stayed.

Diligently, Aisha began to tie the scarves together and measured them.

'Chamsa mitr. Five meters. We must have at least chamsien mitr, fifty meters,' she told her son, who now stood with his back to her. He looked down to the water in the River Darro swirling with foam whitecaps. There was something weak, immature, and insecure in his face, but I thought I saw a look of revenge in his eyes too.

'Your father is a tyrant, boy. We must fight him, and you will become the greatest ruler of Granada.'

'But I don't want that, ummi.'

'You are still young, ibni. The Nasrid blood flows through your veins, and you will defeat the Christians. By Allah, I will personally see to that.'

The boy turned around and responded to her: 'I'm not a fighter. I'm afraid.'

His words confirmed my feelings, and I recognized something in him. The son was no match for the commanding hand of the mother.

'Nonsense. Help me make those knots.'

Rashid came in again with more rags. 'All your servants have given their scarves, Melika. The sultan will not notice. Tonight, Ahmed and Musta will have the horses ready on the riverbank.'

'Sukran, Rashid.' Aisha nodded at him and reached into the bundle of soft silk for a new scarf. Now, aided by Boabdil, she industriously knotted the escape rope. They didn't speak anymore.

I studied the mother with her son and saw myself: a boy slumped in a chair with pimples and a bored look in his eyes.

My elbows rested on the armrests, my forearms stuck up, and my hands moved along the uncoiled yarn of hand-spun sheep's wool. The slight smell of urine and sheep fat tickled my nostrils.

'Come on, Jacob, go faster! Tomorrow I have to start on that weaving commission,' said Inez's voice in my head. Our apartment was full of baskets of unspun sheep's wool, twined yarn, and knotted wool. When I got home from school, Inez was either spinning at an old spinning wheel or sitting behind her weaving loom.

When we lived in Israel, Inez knew some shepherds from whom she got the wool. She drove the jeep into the desert, where we met them. I remember the almost Biblical pictures of nomads with their flocks grazing behind the tents. The sheep chewing on some straw, stared at us, white, wealthy Europeans. As if they knew we would all reincarnate into sheep one day. Back then, I liked those trips with Inez. Later, when we lived in Hackney, she got the wool from a shop in Scotland, a lot less romantic. On our balcony, the strands of spun and washed wool hung on the clothesline to dry. The colors ochre, sienna, lime green and salmon pink, dyed with walnut husk, onion skin and currant juice are still vividly in my mind. And yet, in spite of everything, when I was holding her wool, those nights were cosy.

'Your father never had time for this. He found my knitting and weaving mania embarrassing. It was crazy, of course, in that heat. Yet I've always sold everything. I didn't do it for money, then. Now I have to. Jacob, are you listening?'

'Yes, yes.' I sat up a little more.

'Your father was brimming with money but never bought

anything nice for himself, nor for me.'

'But you didn't care, did you?'

'Oh no, I don't care about luxury. Money doesn't buy happiness.'

'Unless you have it.'

'No. Your father had money, but we weren't happy.' Inez thought it was because of his money that their marriage ended. It became a source of quarrels, which often went nowhere, only evoking mutual irritations and reproaches, incomprehension, and mistrust.

'You didn't fit together?'

'But I loved him, Jacob.'

'Why?'

'His pretty grey eyes, his smile, his jokes.'

'That's not enough.'

'He needed me.'

'Peter and William needed you, and you crawled into his bed and conceived me.'

'How do you know that?'

'I was there myself.'

That made her laugh, and at that point, the conversation took a turn. She wasn't talking about dad anymore; she started to talk about me. God, these conversations we had. I was so tired of them all.

I was looking back into my youth but was in the Alhambra. Confused, I grabbed at the rainbow-colored rope of scarves that hung through the tower, those bright red, blue and yellow fascinated me. I rubbed my face against it, wanted to feel the softness, sniff the scent. Smell my mother again.

I felt a hard tap on my fingers and looked up. Had Aisha

noticed me after all?

'Get off.' An American woman's voice bleated in my face. Two bright red lips parted, square yellow teeth glittering between them. My knees poked into the marble of the floor. My gaze drifted along the colorful pattern of her skirt and T-shirt. She yelled at me. The man next to her looked grey as an elephant to me. Together they pushed me away. The fabric of her skirt slipped from my fingers. A burning wave of nausea swept through me, and I tried to get up. Someone grabbed my arm and threw me out of the tower, out of the palace.

I staggered next to someone to a bench and was pushed down. A woman in uniform shook my shoulder and yelled in my ear: 'Ticket, ticket?'

Slowly I came to my senses. I waved my hands, gesturing I didn't have one. Showed my pockets inside out. I lost it, I gestured. Curious tourists shuffled past. The movement, the ringing in my ears, it all became too much, and again, my stomach flared up to my throat. I gasped but didn't throw up.

'Toda va bien,' I managed to say, 'no pasa nada.' I learned that from Angel when he reassured his dogs. I repeated it until the officer shrugged and walked away.

Slowly, I recovered, and the images came back. I had witnessed an intimacy between a mother and her son, which intertwined with memories of my own mother. I wanted to leave the bench, but my legs seemed filled with lead. People swarmed around me like wasps, and I waited. My tongue felt like leather blocking the entrance to my throat. The water bottle I always carried in my backpack was empty. I tried to orientate myself, but everything was in a fog. Where had that uniform put me? For now, I decided not to move and closed my eyes.

I was back in the tower. It was evening, and I saw how Aisha clambered out of the low window, carefully but resolute. She slipped along the cord of scarves down the tower's coarse, reddish-brown stone wall. Then Boabdil followed her. Below, on the bank of the swirling river, stood two men with white turbans next to two horses. They helped Aisha on one, and Boabdil mounted the other horse. The next moment, the horses, with their royal cargo, vanished like shadows in the night; their clop-clop audible on the riverbank.

I opened my eyes and felt better. It had been good to finish the scene, to live it through. I could now see the bystanders, who sauntered past, clearly. I turned my head to the right, and there, ten meters from me flowed the water of a fountain. Wobbly, I stepped over and drank the lukewarm water. It helped. My tongue shrunk. My mouth and lips felt more normal again. With both hands, I splashed water on my face.

What time would it be? I didn't wear a watch; I lived on my own time and kept an eye on the sun. But now I didn't feel in my body what time it was. I didn't feel hungry and didn't know if it was nearly lunchtime. The Mediterranean sun was too bright and hard to focus on. The sun at ten, twelve or four o'clock was much of the same here.

Behind me, a man waited patiently. I didn't see him until I straightened up, my eyes sliding to his wrist. I saw the hands on his watch and was startled. I leaned towards him because I didn't believe what I saw. When he was finished, I asked if his watch was fast.

'Nein, es ist genau viertel vor sechs.'

Quarter to six. Three hours late for my meeting with Sam. This was terrible. As best as I could, I hurried to the bus stop, and walked past an empty taxi. I changed my mind. Better idea. I knocked on the window and mentioned the name of the restaurant where I should have met Sam hours ago. The driver nodded; I opened the door and sank into the cool leather of the back seat.

The restaurant turned out to be closed. On a menu next door, I read it would be open again at nine o'clock. I guessed Sam would have gone back to the hotel, so I went there. She was not in our room, but paper bags with designer clothes and shoes stood in the corner. Sooner or later, she would come back. I fell onto the bed and fell into a deep sleep.

Hours later, or just a few minutes, Sam woke me up. Furious and worried.

'By five o'clock, I was so worried, I went to the Alhambra to inquire if there had been an accident. Nobody knew anything. I would have gone to the police if you weren't here now.'

It was difficult to keep my eyes open, while I massaged my heavy eyelids.

'What have you done?' She rattled to me. 'You went to a pub and got drunk?'

I shook my head.

'You definitely look like it. Your eyes are bloodshot, and you stink.'

I meekly nodded yes. I couldn't fight back without strength. I felt like Boabdil helping his domineering mother tie scarves. Or, was I the boy who was supposed to be holding up his mother's wool while the boys next door played soccer? I slumped back into the pillow and faced my mother with a clenched fist. I didn't want her to command me, I couldn't take it anymore, but I put my fist in my pocket and obeyed.

'Come on, what else is there?' Sam had brushed her teeth and came out of the bathroom.

'Forgotten the time, sorry.'

Seething at my absent-mindedness, she crawled beside me.

'What have you bought, Squirrel,' I tried sweetly.

'Shoes, a summer dress at Zara, sexy underwear.'

'Was it fun?'

'Was okay. I sat on a terrace, wrote cards, watched people.'

I yawned and went for a pee. Startled, I looked at my face in the mirror. Thick, heavy eyes and a slightly swollen tongue.

'Sleep tight.' I kissed Sam's cheek guiltily; she lay on her side, reading. She had been distraught. Luckily, she was still angry enough not to want anything from me or to look at me closely.

Laying on my back, I stared at the vaguely moving shadows at the ceiling. At last, I had the peace to reflect on my experience. How could I have been physically present in the past, with them, in their time? Did that mean that my time travels weren't spiritual after all? I shook my head: Impossible. After all my body had stayed in today's world. The mixture of sage and oil and something else made me just highly receptive to spheres.

Inez was very spiritual orientated. Sam, fortunately, was more down to earth. But now I longed for my mother, in her polychrome rags and self-knitted cardigans, flowing skirts and henna-dyed hair, she would understand my investigation into the past. She believed in reincarnation. We smoked joints together. 'Jacob,' she said, 'you see, what I see?' In a trance, she shared her visualisations with me. 'I am walking in a blue forest, the sky is green, and the ground is red.'

'I think you read too many psychedelic books.' Then we laughed together.

Later, in the late 1970s, the colors of her clothes turned monochromatic: warm red, orange or pink. She went to Poona and became a follower of Bhagwan. In the nineties, she converted to Buddhism. These days she is a shaman and wears only white.

Sam ridiculed her, which annoyed me. I defended Inez and felt like the boy who had to protect her against my father. She had become a tragic figure always looking for recognition and friendship from the wrong people, and always making the wrong decisions. Now, as a practising shaman, she has acquired a certain status. She knows how to help people and provide relief, which is her way to deal with loneliness.

I went to an international school in Italy for five years. My two half-brothers had preceded me. It was an expensive but good school. In the holidays I went home. I still remember that summer when things went horribly wrong between my parents. Peter was just eighteen and picked me up from the airport in Jerusalem. Grinning, he warned me: 'Those two will punch each other in the head.'

He left the next day, happy to go his own way, leaving me at the mercy of two hostile parents. I wished I could follow Peter, but I was only nine.

Dad barely showed up. Inez went out of her way to please

me. After two days, I saw dad come out of Rachel's house. He nodded to me like I was a stranger and ignored Inez and me for the next few days. I'll never forget, it was then that I decided: I didn't want kids. The holiday lasted and lasted. Relieved, I went back to boarding school. The anonymity of those long corridors, the high, chilly classrooms, the distant monks, and the vague friendships were more attractive than parents who behaved childishly and resentful.

Halfway through the first trimester, after that summer, I was in class and literally, Inez, draped in scarves, sailed into the classroom, and that same afternoon we were on a plane from Milan to London. I never said goodbye to the friends I had finally made and who were, meanwhile, dearer to me than those parents.

I was sixteen when Inez went to Poona, and I had to stay with my father in Nice. Still, I have no bad memories of that time. I went sailing with William. Rachel felt sorry for me, and dad kept his distance.

I was a grumpy adolescent. William, by then twenty-eight, had a girlfriend in Saint-Tropez and saw my unhappiness. One day we were sailing. I sat at the bottom of the boat, tying knots, showing no interest in the blue water, the distant mountains or the warm wind blowing around my head.

William said: 'It's not you, it's dad. I also had my problems with him.' I looked up. Could that big brother be an ally?

'When Inez came to our house, dad blossomed,' William said. 'She was twenty-two, dad an old, gloomy man who'd shut himself up. He had problems with the embassy and missed my mother. He felt guilty and responsible for her death.'

'How did that actually happen?'

'He was going to pick us up from a children's party, but something came up, so my mother went, though she was seven months pregnant. She overtook a car without seeing the oncoming traffic in the low afternoon light. What I remember from that day is the waiting. Hours and hours later, Rachel came to pick us up. She was the messenger who told us our mother and her unborn child were dead.'

'I didn't know about the baby.'

'No? It would have been a little sister. Dad was a wreck, of course. But after a few months, he decided to carry on again. For Peter and me and his social status he needed a new wife.'

'Inez told me he came on a working visit to the kibbutz and proposed to her right there,' I said.

'Inez working in a kibbutz in the early 1960's was progressive. But she was like that, a spontaneous girl who loved to sing and act,' said William. 'I was twelve and secretly in love with her.'

'Really?' I suddenly looked at my half-brother with different eyes.

'Yeah, she was my first love, but she was just motherly to us, you know, she only had eyes for dad. She managed to free him from his gloomy, dour grief. He wasn't very social, but she was. He drowned in his work. Inez cheered him up, all of us, as we missed our mother too.'

'They got married because she was expecting me,' I said. 'William, do you think dad loved her?'

'At first, yes. But when you came, he probably compared you with the unborn baby girl.' I swallowed. Was that it? Was I the dead girl's surrogate?

'But you were already at boarding school in Italy, weren't you?'

'Yes, but we came to stay during the holidays. I longed for that; I wanted to be with Inez again. But she had you, her toy. She no longer had eyes for me, and I became jealous.'

'And I was jealous of you. Dad treated you and Peter like his true sons.'

'Misunderstandings make people unhappy.'

'Nobody talked or said what they thought.'

'It was a superficial life, with parties and dances, the luxurious life. Inez was a good hostess, and she was good with the servants.'

'She made my clothes herself, which I hated. I always felt like I was on stage in a costume,' I said.

'She loved acting.' William grinned. His hair fluttered in the wind as he swerved a little.

'Later, she got into Tarot, I Ching, and then astrology, dad wouldn't have none of it.'

'Your mother was losing her grip on dad and us.'

'And therefore, she clung to me.'

I didn't remember much of the rest of the conversation other than tightening the jib and leaning boldly overboard to keep the boat straight.

Pa could no longer stand Inez's capriciousness; he increasingly sought the peace of neighbor Rachel. Her husband died, and dad comforted her. Finally, he sent Inez and me away. It took him a lot of effort to get rid of her. My mother was not easily turned away. He had bought that apartment in Hackney, which he put in my name. Inez was bitter, angry, and disappointed. We struggled financially, but she made it. She taught drama in primary schools and wove beautiful fabrics from her self-spun and dyed wool. And she was always knitting those damned itchy sweaters. In London, I went to secondary school and went my own way as much as possible.

The following summer, I was seventeen, and I returned to Nice. I was now sailing alone in William's boat. I liked Rachel, but I barely got in touch with dad.

'He's so sullen and never laughs at my jokes,' I once said desperately to Rachel.

'I know, and it makes you miserable, but he can't. He sees Inez in you.'

'But I'm not my mother. Dammit, I want to be his son.' Furious, I ran away and sailed out with the boat; I stayed away for two days. When I returned, he said nothing and kicked me into my room.

That phone call, a month before I turned twenty-one, was his victory. Of course, it touched me. For the first time, we had a real conversation over the phone, without interference from Inez or Rachel.

In the years after his death, I realised I had missed a father, an example, a friend and a counsellor. I couldn't change it anymore. It was how it was. I had to come to terms with that.

I wondered if the sage would bring me back to my own childhood. Now I was rummaging through Boabdil's life. Wouldn't it help me to shake dad's hand again, give him a warm hug, and try to understand him?

Sam had fallen asleep over her book. I bent over her, pulled it from her hands, put it on the nightstand next to her, and flipped out the bedside lamp. Lying on my side, I stared into the darkness, thinking about the effects of the Sage of the Ghosts and my growing need to go back in time. What sort of feelings did Boabdil have towards his father? He also had a demanding mother and missed opportunities with his father and half-brothers.

'It's not for nothing that you come across this, Jacob. You must deal with it,' I heard Inez say. She was probably right.

LOJA

The Alcazaba

*T*he next day, I felt reasonably fit. Sam demanded my attention for the everyday things, and I hardly thought about my experiences in the Alhambra. Our drive to Seville was on the agenda and we took our time. Sam wanted to show me a special shop window and I still wanted to visit Ferdinand and Isabella in the Capilla Real, the tomb of the Catholic Monarchs. By one o'clock we drove out of the city. Sam sat behind the wheel. I was fine with that; the thought of driving disgusted me. I wouldn't have been able to concentrate on that right now. Besides, if she was driving, she wouldn't pay much attention to me.

As soon as we were on the highway, I lost myself in the undulating landscape between the endless rows of olive trees in white-grey earth. In the distance, the earth was laced with rusty ochre tones and misty shapes of bluish ridges shimmering against the sky. As we got closer, they turned out to be solid reddish-brown rocks. The heavy shadows gave shape and texture to the mountains.

From time to time, I felt Sam's gaze resting on me. I pretended not to notice. She was clearly worried since my disappearance the previous day. However, she didn't ask me anything.

Plunged in thought, I was back in the tower watching mother and son. I had no words for my experience: just feelings, deep feelings. I did not exist. I was insignificant, a pinprick in this universe. A nobody, who only was himself. A deep, sad loneliness came over me. I needed someone to take me by the hand. Five hundred years ago, a vital energy had flowed through me, but in the present, I felt nothing but cold and empty. Had I lost my soul? Way back in that other world, had I been Boabdil? I sat up straight. What an absurd fantasy. Me, Boabdil? He had been deeply unhappy and was a puppet in a joust of bigotry, religion, and power. I didn't want to be him at all. Although? Didn't we now live exactly in such a world where religion and ideology still had a lot of influence on politics in some cultures.

I must have let out a deep sigh, because next to me Sam asked: 'Are you okay?'

'Fine. I was just thinking, what a good thing religion would be, if politics wouldn't interfere. If there was only beauty, love, and spirituality in our world, like in Buddhism or Sufism.'

'Is that what you were thinking? To me your mind seemed to be more prosaic,' she said smiling.

'And how refreshing would Islam be without the interference of politics,' I went on pretending not noticing her cynicism.

'Ah well, and what about the power of money. It will always be that way; history shows us that anyway.'

Looking at her sideways, I said: 'Money is not the issue now. The fact that Christianity is disconnected from politics makes us freer in the West. In Islam, the Ayatollahs and Taliban still have a major influence on politics. That is fundamentally wrong, I think.'

At a road sign announcing the next turn, I realised we were approaching Loja. This was Morayma's place of birth. At the time, her father was the mayor here. My heart skipped a beat, I would love to nose around in Loja.

It was almost two o'clock, lunch time. Not that I had to think about food, but when Sam's blood sugar dropped, she got cranky.

'Let's have lunch here, Squirrel.'

'Good idea. I am hungry and it is nice to stretch our legs.'

'There must be some remains of a Moorish castle here, I would love to see that.'

'There's a mesón, even better.' Sam parked in front of a restaurant, sandwiched between a couple of stores, already closed for siesta.

I chose a table from the many rows and stared mindlessly at the green and white checked tablecloths.

'Would you really, want to explore more ruins?' Sam came

back from the toilet, hung her backpack over the back of the chair and sat down opposite me. 'Have you seen one, you have seen them all, right?'

'It's always something else for me.'

'What then? You are a history freak, I know, but tell me what's so important about those piled up stones.'

'Gosh Sam, why so cynical?'

'Cynical? Do you think that's cynical? You mainly live in your own world. You don't ask me anything, you either find me a bore or I resemble my mother. And you never want to talk about my desire to have children.'

I heaved a deep sigh. My god, there we go again, I thought the danger had passed. 'You're right,' I said peacefully, but a little too quickly.

'You see. You avoid confrontation, joining the conversation without arguing.'

'Why would I want to argue? I'm not into that at all. I'm just trying to be smart.'

'No, you're not.'

'I am an individualist. Not suitable for family life, I don't even know what it is. I'm interested in you, but not in those shoes with those cute heels, you didn't buy after all. Sorry, Squirrel, but I don't care about things, and you know that damn well.'

She bit her lip, held her tongue for a moment, then asked: 'What fascinates you so much about those ancient times?'

'That we come from something that has been. We are the same as our ancestors. They once were, now we are.'

'They were, now we are? Is that all you care about? I thought I had you pretty well sorted out, but this is sheer nonsense.'

'If only...,' I tried and shut my mouth. The waiter stood next to us and quickly read a whole row of dishes from a piece of paper. When we'd made our choice, he disappeared between the tables.

In less than no time, the guy returned with two plates of Gazpacho. We ate the cold tomato soup in silence, while I watched the television in the corner of the hall. Even before we had finished our soup, he brought the main course. I poked listlessly into limp fries and cut a piece of pork with the texture of a shoe sole.

Even before Sam had finished her plate, she started again, persistently as she was: 'Jacob, really, I want a child so badly. Can't we agree? I promise I will do everything. I understand perfectly well that you don't like a pooping and screaming pink piglet. My brother always says that they become fun when they start walking and chatting, then you get in touch with them.'

'I don't want the responsibility.'

'I'm three months without an IUD, it could just work now.'

I sighed again. 'Hopefully my semen is infertile.'

She looked shocked. 'Bastard. Why do we always have to argue about this?'

'Sam, the thought of children paralyzes me, I have them in my classes, I like them there. But my own child? I wouldn't know how to handle that. My parents didn't know it either. At least I'm glad I'm aware of that. How many people start a family without thinking.'

'I know what I'm doing. I've thought it over many times.'

The waiter removed our plates, and asked: 'Postre?'

'Cafe solo,' I said.

'Gosh, Prick, you've hardly eaten anything, and you were so hungry, you said.'

'I didn't say that, you said you were hungry.'

After the coffee, we stepped outside, the heat hit me in the face, and Sam stepped briskly to the driver's side of the car.

'Come on, let's go to the Alcazaba.' I pointed above us. 'There it is on that rock, we'll be there in a minute.'

'Hey? But it is almost four o'clock and we still want to go to Seville.'

'Just a minute, come on. We have all the time, right? We are on holiday, remember?'

Grumbling, she drove up the steep, winding road to the tourist attraction above the city. We got out in a deserted parking lot, the wind blowing warm in our faces. The ruin consisted of a tower, some piles of stones and crumbling walls, which had clearly been restored by modern human hands. From here we had a great view at Loja below us in the valley, and by now in the afternoon partly in the shade. The city was surrounded by barren mountains, with here and there trees grouped around white spots of lonely houses, shimmering in the afternoon light. There was not much to see at the ruin, but I tasted the atmosphere of the past. Boabdil had walked here; I felt his energy. I tried to visualise him and considered to take a few crumbs of the sage.

Sam sat on a wall, reading a fist-thick novel, not showing any interest in the surroundings, she clearly cut her losses.

In a quiet place I looked for the box in my backpack. Once I got hold of it, I studied the Arabic characters on the lid carefully, as if they contained the answer to all my questions.

I opened it and studied the sage paste. The color seemed

to be more green than brown. I tore off a piece. Too slow. Sam's voice approached: 'Jacob, where are you? Come on, it's after five. We need to go to Seville.'

I quickly put the box back in the backpack and called: 'Let's find a hotel! I like it here.'

'I don't! We were supposed to be in Seville today. Now our whole travel program is messed up.'

'What difference does it make?' Back at the car, I flipped through the travel guide and found Loja. 'There is a hotel with a swimming pool and a jacuzzi. What do you think of that?'

Sam loved to swim, and my suggestion was bull's eye.

We got a nice room at the back of Hotel 'El Mirador' with a view of the Alcazaba. Everything was luxurious, and Sam's mood improved by the minute. She dove into the pool and splashed merrily around me. I took it easy, my rock-hard muscles reacted like rusty hinges to oil. They relaxed somewhat in the lukewarm chloride water, until my skin started to tingle. For a moment it was a pleasant sensation, but soon it started to sting as if I were rolling through a field of nettles. I shot out of the water and dried myself off, so hard my skin turned red and rough. But I came back to myself.

At the bar, under the obtrusive television, we ate a plate of fresh anchovies. That is to say, Sam ate most of the fish. After a few glasses of country wine, which was easy to drink but quickly rose to our head, we crawled into our king-size bed. The air conditioner buzzed overhead. Sam's hand slid between my legs. Her thumb made a massaging motion, but too drowsy, I turned away and fell asleep.

Boabdil meets Morayma

After midnight I woke up with a bad taste in my mouth. I jumped out of bed, gargled my throat with Sam's Listerine and conceived a plan. I put on my shorts and pulled my T-shirt over my head. The light of the nearly full moon shone through the curtains. In the distance the Alcazaba, lit by orange floodlights, beckoned me. My backpack lay like a pathetic grey heap on a chair. I reached for the box and put it in my pocket.

Outside the room, I remembered the car keys in Sam's pocket and went back. She slept soundly and deeply, hopefully I would be back before she woke up. In the dimly lit hotel corridor, my sandals sank into the deep-pile carpet. The elevator whizzed down. The luxurious entrance, we admired this afternoon, was dimly lit by energy-saving lamps, the reception desk was shuttered.

The car stood around the corner. Starting the engine sounded like a bombing raid in the still night. Slightly guilty, I drove through the empty streets back to the Alcazaba. I parked the car in the abandoned parking lot. It had been the only one a few hours ago, and it was the only one now. My shadow moved along the walls like a magnified bulky shape. It was dead silent, until the cry of an owl tore the night apart. A dry breeze brushed my head. Despite the floodlights and the moonlight, I saw stars in the sky.

Sitting on the crumbling wall, I took a good chunk of the waxy Sage of the Ghosts and let it melt under my tongue. This would be the fourth time. I felt tense and walked around a bit, waiting for what was to come. I peered at the town below me. Suppose someone was walking down the street, a policeman for instance, looking up at this moment, could he see my dancing shadows on the walls?

Overwhelmed by fear of being caught, I lay down and closed my eyes. Immediately a birthday party occurred to me. I was five or six. Inez sat in front of a white sheet and performed a shadow play for my friends. She projected with her hands a hopping bunny, chased by an angry fox in a scary forest, imitating the funny voices. I was the birthday boy and sat proudly between the big-eyed and open-mouthed kids Me, the little prince with a colored paper crown on his head. We were pulled into the fairy-tale world, my mother conjured up for me and my friends. What a heart-warming memory, I thought happily.

The night closed in on me, aware of myself on that pile of old stones, I heard a high-pitched tone buzzing in my ears. Was this it? Had I only gone forty years back in time? Wasn't that a wonderful idea? Being back in my own childhood. Reliving that time, the happy moments, meeting my father and half-brothers again?

The stones shook beneath me. A drumming of horse hooves came near. I narrowed my eyes as the sky slowly changed color. I felt time slip by. On and on, I went back. Back to the past. Back to the Moor. Finally. I had lived my youth. I wanted to meet Boabdil. I longed for him. I stared in the direction of the swelling sound and saw two figures, who broke free from a cloud of dust and two beautiful Arabian horses rushed up the hill.

I jumped up. The wall had not crumbled at all, the wall I'd

sat on was the sill of a large window with thick iron bars. Behind it, I saw an open courtyard with orange trees. The horses snorted and I admired their shiny, black skin and colorful halters. Over one horse hung a cloth decorated with gold thread and turquoise stitching. The rider stood with his back to me and tied the reins to an iron ring in the wall. He brushed off the dust of his indigo cape and poured water into his mouth from a leather bag. When he turned around, I recognized Boabdil. My sultan. Only a little older than when he was with his mother in the tower, but many years younger than the tired, broken man I had met at Angel's inn. For a moment, he squinted through the low evening light at where they came from, where the dust, which almost looked like golden powder, whirled to the ground. Beyond that, the city of Loja was barely discernible.

'Ahmed, take care of the horses, we'll go back to Granada tonight.'

He stepped past me to the huge copper-clad gate a few yards to our left. His silk cape billowed behind him. I followed, without hesitation making sure I didn't touch anything. After my experience in the Alhambra with the American woman, I knew the spell would break, as soon as I touched the gleaming blue splendor of his cape.

'Salaam aleikhum.' Boabdil greeted the two guards who bowed to him. Apparently, he was a respected man here. A small door in the huge gate opened and he stepped into the courtyard I had seen behind the window. It was a square space, surrounded by a one-meter-wide gallery, supported by slender columns. Geometric shadows fell on the marble tiles.

Boabdil stopped and looked. I followed his gaze between two rows of orange trees, which were connected by a shallow gutter in the pavement. I heard the sound of gurgling water.

A sonorous buzz, and a repeated beep caught Boabdil's attention. He looked intently at a girl behind a spinning wheel. Her hair danced on her back to the beat of her regular kicking foot. A gold band glittered around her ankle. A dab of silk left her hand, disappeared behind the wheel, and reappeared like a thin, shiny thread, before being twisted on a spool. We stood together, stirred, looking at her slender grace.

He waited. Probably, hoping the girl could sense his presence, so that she would turn around. As if experiencing it myself, he went through the stages of falling in love: admiration for her simple beauty, unconditional devotion and surrender, mixed with uncertainty, and a feeling of here she is, she, who must belong to me! But I also sensed doubt, what would he say, as she looked up. His emotions were mine. His eyes were mine. I felt the same affection for her. We were one.

She, sitting between the trunks of orange trees, became aware of our energy drifting towards her. Her foot stopped, the whirring wheel turned more and more slowly, till it stopped. I no longer heard the soft tinkling bells around her ankle. She lifted her face as we stepped into the light and looked into her eyes. Just eyes. Clear blue pools with a staggering depth. A tinge of terror passed over her face, then surprise, then pleasure, and her heart-shaped face burst into a radiant smile. The girl was fully aware of Boabdil's confusion.

However, he recovered quickly, nodded a bit rigidly, and crossed the court to the side wing. Where was he going? I hurried after him, cast one last glance over my shoulder, and saw a fine smile on the girl's lips.

We walked through a labyrinth of corridors, not as richly and delicately decorated as in the Alhambra, but they radiated the same high culture and good taste. Unbelievable, that those rough, robust walls concealed so much beauty inside. We were on our way to Ali Atar, the mayor of Loja, widower and the father of the young girl, Morayma. At least, that's what I suspected because this was his castle. He was a feared warlord, highly regarded by his own people. Even the Christians respected him, for winning many battles from them.

Ali Atar rose from behind his table when we entered the room. A tall, thin man in his fifties, wearing a dark red turban and a lighter red woolen robe. Sharp eyes poked watchfully from beneath two bushy eyebrows. He was clearly pleased to see Boabdil.

'Ibni, son,' he said informally, 'long time no see, what can I do for you.'

'Sayyid, my lord.' Boabdil began with a slight hesitation in his voice. 'As I am officially king, since my father has been imprisoned, and the people of Granada have elected me as their leader...'

The old man nodded impatiently.

'But you know, I detest this war? I am no warrior. I have ideals, but I will never be able to realise them in this world. I see the human being behind the enemy, because in essence we are all equal, with our need for love, recognition, and happiness. Fighting negates all those wishes. Fighting causes hatred and division.'

The old man thoughtfully stroked his pointed beard: 'It is too late for such noble thoughts, Ibni. The Christians are determined to overrule Islam. They are bloodthirsty. They'll fight until the last drop of blood has shed. They want power and domination.'

'I must show my people that I will never surrender Granada. I don't want to capitulate; I want to resist without fighting.'

'You can't.' Ali Atar shook his head seriously. 'You can count on my support, my army...' A soft tap on the door interrupted the conversation.

Boabdil bowed his head and threw the cape around his shoulder with an uncertain gesture. The girl came in. On a tray she carried a pitcher and two glasses. This time she was veiled, but her eyes, those two blue lakes, were uncovered.

'Muhammad, this is my daughter, Morayma. You know of her existence, but I don't believe you've ever met?'

'No, Sayyid.' Boabdil took the tray from her hands and set it on a small table. The cape slipped from his shoulder, and the way he wrapped it again, that impatient gesture, betrayed his uncertainty.

Morayma's eyes were smiling, meaning she could control this man. Ali Atar saw it too. His hawk eyes missed nothing. Their love blossomed before our eyes; its intensity moved me.

With a slight bow, without saying a word, she disappeared again.

Boabdil recovered quickly, faster than I did, and resumed

the conversation with Ali Atar. I understood that the man promised him full military support against the army of Ferdinand and Isabella.

Their conversation came to an end. Boabdil hesitated, licked his lips, took another sip of water, threw the cape back on his shoulder, coughed behind his hand, shuffled the tip of his boot over a ledge in a flagstone, then asked begrudgingly: 'Isn't your daughter too much alone here? May I visit her again?'

Amazed, I listened to Ali Atar's direct reply. 'You're asking for her hand? Son, you have my blessing. You are a good man, a brave man, and a king. Why don't you ask her yourself? I want her to marry for love, just like I chose her mother.'

Both men left the room and walked back to the patio. I crept along the wall in their shadows, though I didn't have to worry, they wouldn't sense my presence.

This time, Morayma sat next to the softly splashing fountain with some embroidery on her lap. She didn't hear us approaching and was visibly startled as Boabdil's shadow fell over her. She pricked herself, let out a soft squeak and put her finger in her mouth, her eyes darting uncertainly from her father to Boabdil. She hesitated; did she only now realise who this man was? Shyly, she lowered her gaze as Boabdil kept looking at her. Neither of them noticed her father had silently sneaked away. Morayma, slowly raised her eyes again, and for several long seconds their gaze interlocked until their souls fused together.

She was the first to be distracted. Her gaze wandered down his body, past his silk tunic, his trousers and soft leather boots, which were dusty, but elegant. Then back over his face, past his angular, bony cheekbones, his shimmering black hair behind his ears. His nose was a little bit big. His mouth a straight line, giving him something hard and unapproachable, a disguise of his true feelings, I knew. Morayma, seeing his brown eyes turn tender and soft, discovered that instant, his vulnerability too.

Again, he threw the cape over his shoulder. She didn't know yet how well she would get to know, love and hate, that gesture. That gesture hid his anger and frustration, impatience and indecision, his ruthlessness, and his deepest emotions. She stood up, the blue dress falling slender and straight along her body. The previously, carefully draped veil had slipped down, when she had put her finger in her mouth, now the scarf lay casually around her shoulders. Tens of golden bells tinkled softly on the satin cord around her hips. Her light-colored, wide-eyed face, framed by the golden-red hair, reminded me of a freshly-opened flower.

Boabdil briefly looked around to make sure they were alone and took her hand. He gently pulled the finger out of her mouth, briefly massaged the sore spot with his thumb, then stuck her finger into his own mouth. A glimmer of a smile drove the previous serious look from his eyes, as he gently bit her finger.

She returned his smile, full and open.

The next moment, they laughed heartily, carefree and in love. And I, witness of this blossoming love, relaxed. Their warmth also flowed through my body, endeared me too. I wanted to feel her too, touch her, look into her eyes, but the moment passed. Boabdil broke away from her and disappeared into the shadows. Quickly I turned around, I had to follow him, but I was too late. The wooden gate slammed shut in front of me, and in an incredible way I hit my head and fell on the ground.

I opened my eyes with difficulty, I lay in an uncomfortable position on the sand. My knee had a painful abrasion, and a lump the size of a pigeon's egg grew on my head. It was still dark, but dawn was glimmering in the east, in the direction where the two men had gone, back to Granada. I'd been in the past for nearly four hours, though it seemed much longer, now the effect of the sage had totally vanished.

I took a few steps, afraid of the wave of nausea that would overtake me, but nothing happened. Apart from the graze on my knee, I felt good. No, that wasn't true, I felt better than ever. I felt disembodied, exalted, satisfied.

Even in the darkness, I saw how the wall, I had bumped my head against so mercilessly, must be of a later date. The grout was of a different quality. Between two old sandstone columns, the space of about three meters wide was bricked up with a new stone wall. These columns seemed to have once effortlessly supported a heavy door. My fantasy claimed, this was indeed the gateway to Ali Atar's castle.

Deep in thought, I sauntered over to the car and got behind the wheel. I slowly drove back to the hotel, completely unaware of my current situation. But I was full of thoughts of Morayma, who with her uninhibited, warm gaze had unleashed a deep love in me.

On the key ring, there were two keys, one for our room, the second key fitted on the outside door of the hotel. I slipped inside, sneaking past the dark lobby and I had no idea where to go. Usually, Sam took the initiative, and I just followed her. On the key ring, I read number 303. Oh yes, third floor. In the elevator I looked for the three and as in a dream I found the door to our room.

Somewhat tense as to what condition I would find my girlfriend in, I stepped inside. Was she waiting for me? Dressed, furious and worried? Or was she naked between the sheets, with a lovely smile on her lips? To my surprise, she was just sleeping. Her hair was like a red-golden halo around her face. I quickly undressed and slid between the sheets next to her. The warmth of her body drew me to her. My hands hugged her buttocks, slid down her thighs, down her silky legs. Slowly, I crawled along her limbs, my lips against her skin, until my nose landed somewhere in the soft vault between her thighs. Softly moaning, she let me go on.

She snuggled close to me with a sigh. 'Jacob,' I heard, 'Jacob.'

That name meant nothing to me at all. Under my massaging thumb, her body writhed like a mermaid in a warm sea. Her legs hugged my lower body, and she waved around me. We found the right rhythm, and together we rocked to the peak. I didn't know this existed.

My scream drowned out hers. Slowly, I felt my semen pour into her like an army of soldiers facing the enemy.

I opened my eyes and expected to look into Morayma's dark blue pools. Instead, I saw brown dots in a soft green, cloudy look. I fell back into the pillows, unaware of what I had just done, and fell into a deep sleep.

Burst of rage

The next moment I rode on horseback to Granada. I took the outside route to the Alhambra so that I wouldn't have to cross the city and be held up by my subjects. They usually forced me to stop to accept gifts and friendly exclamations, which I received with a slight bow and the necessary words of thanks. I passed the Gate of Justice and disappeared - unseen - into the palace; where, to make matters worse, my mother was waiting for me.

'What happened to you?' She saw immediately that I was in a different mood than this morning when I left for Loja. I resisted her compelling gaze, usually I answered my mother's questions, even in her ruthless tone. I now remained silent, which aroused her even more. She totally controlled my feelings and decisions, but that had to end, right now! After all, I was the king.

I opened my mouth, starting to tell her plainly... when Sam shook me awake. 'Jacob, get up, I already had a swim, I want to go to Seville.'

I moaned and turned reluctantly to my side, away from her. I mused on, but the spell was broken. What a strange dream. I was Boabdil, but the mother was not Aisha from the Comares Tower. On the contrary, she was Inez, my own mother.

I dragged myself out of bed and felt just as tense as yesterday. I showered, put on clean clothes, and hardly felt any better. We left the room and Sam demonstratively clung to me, she stroked my cheek and wanted to kiss me. I patted her on the back, as if she were a strange woman who just learned her husband had passed away.

Down in the breakfast room, another tourist couple sat at a table in the corner. I followed Sam to the bar and stared blankly at the blaring television. Sam leafed through a Spanish newspaper while we waited for our cafe solos and tostadas.

The first sip seared the taste buds on my tongue. Reflexively, I spat the brown gunk onto the saucer. 'Damn, I'm burning my mouth.'

'But honey, that coffee isn't hot at all, rather on the lukewarm side.' Sam put her hand around my cup, looking at me with concern.

The waiter handed me a napkin and asked if I wanted another cup of coffee. I shook my head, I coughed, tears in my eyes, and pointed to the oranges in a glass container. The man squeezed a fresh glass of juice and put it in front of me at the bar. The sour-sweet orange juice bit into my palate and the insides of my cheeks. I took a bite of my honeyed toast and chewed it as if it was chewing gum. Next to me, Sam poured the golden green olive oil on her toast and topped it with a layer of tomato puree and salt and pepper.

'The ultimate breakfast,' she said, mouthful. 'They all eat this here. Great to start the day with. I'm going to do it at home too. And for 'Kitchen Hands' I'll write an article about international breakfasts with the emphasis on rituals.'

'As long as I can stick to my muesli with yogurt,' I muttered. 'You're funny, you always liked something different,' Sam said.

'It's too early for me, but you're right.' In the mirror behind the bar, visible behind a beer advertisement, the espresso machine, and several bottles of spirits, I watched myself. My short hair stood upright as usual, but the look in my eyes had something desolate. That look worried me; it was as if someone else lived behind my eyes.

'Don't you have to say something?' Sam pushed the newspaper away and put her arm around me. 'What should I say?'

'What got into you last night, honey?'

'Last night?' What had happened? I dug into my memory. I didn't have to go far, because I felt again how I was holding Morayma in my arms.

'You seduced me.'

'I seduced you?'

'Don't you remember? I've never seen you so horny. For a moment I thought you held another woman in your arms.' She laughed like a turtle dove on lover's feet. 'During my fertile period I am always so horny and wet. Jacob, I am so happy. It was perfect, so nice. You know, I even think the conception took place. As a woman you just feel those things.'

For a moment I stared at her in bewilderment, and this time I really choked. I grabbed the napkin. My windpipe was blocked, and it took me a long time to control myself again. Sam slapped me on the back, while I was sneezing and coughing, unable to say anything. With tears dripping along my cheeks, I pointed to the toilet in the lobby and left Sam and the bartender bewildered.

In the toilets, I banged my head against the tiles with Moorish patterns. Stupid. Stupid. Stupid. I had let myself go last night. I had been in that other world. The fact I had not held Morayma in my arms, was a bitter realisation. Of

Sam, I had no memory at all. Had I indeed inseminated her? She was not to blame for this, I really had done this myself. I had lost myself in a dream and arms of another woman. I chewed on my inner cheek, got up and peed. It smelled suspiciously strong. Absently, I staggered back to the bar.

'Prick, why are you so shocked, it was nice last night, wasn't it? Everything is fine with me, don' t worry. Most of it comes down to me anyway. The pregnancy, giving birth, the upbringing. I'm fine with that. I'm a woman.' She laughed deeply and rubbed her belly as if something was already in there. A fertilized egg that would manifest itself in a few moments in a gigantic monstrosity.

'Once the child is here, you will love it too.'

I cringed. 'What? Have you gone mad? Have you decided that for me?' The wild animal inside broke loose. I pulled over the barstool and it clattered thunderously on the flagstones.

The waiter raised his eyebrows. The couple in the corner stood up and left the breakfast room in silence.

Sam put her hand over her mouth and screamed: 'Jacob, what are you doing? Are you crazy?' I strode out of the room, took the elevator upstairs, and went to our room. I looked around, not knowing what else to do, I got my suitcase and backpack. I went to the car, sat behind the wheel, and waited for Sam. For a moment I considered driving away without her, back to Granada. Let her stew in her own juices. She had her child and could go home. Something like that.

Slowly my breathing and my heart rate dropped to normal. I realised I was behaving unreasonably immature. She deserved better. I had to apologise. And immediately a headache began to throb behind my temples.

Sam came out with her suitcase, put it in the trunk, and timidly got in and sat next to me.

We left Loja without a word. On the highway I kicked the Nissan on its tail, but above one hundred and twenty. The whole car started to shake.

'Jacob, we need to talk. There is something very wrong with you and our relationship, we can't solve it this way.'

I shrugged and turned on the radio. Started to hum softly and acted like I was alone in the car. Three hours later we drove into the city. It was one o'clock and the heat scorched the day. This was Seville.

SEVILLE

Reconciliation

Arriving in a new city meant developing new activities: reading the map, parking the car, and looking for a suitable hotel. In those things Sam and I were well attuned to each other. She led me into the city center and I shot the car into a parking area under the Torre del Oro. Expensive, but fine for the moment. We left our luggage in the car and went to look for a hotel. This city felt completely different from pleasant provincial Granada. Here, I was much less in touch with the past, I hardly felt the energy from the descendants of the Nasrid family. Would Boabdil ever have been here? Around 1250 had Seville been already in Christian hands. Thus had a very different past than Granada, which had been ruled by Arab rulers for two hundred and fifty more years.

We found a cheap, but dilapidated hotel next to the wall around the gardens of the Alcazar. The floors in the corridors were so warped, I wondered if it was because of the condition I was in. An annoying air conditioner buzzed in the room, barely bringing the temperature down. I pressed a button and found that the tattered thing had only one setting.

In the afternoon, I reconciled with Sam by apologizing for my unreasonable behavior during breakfast. I went on and on, till Sam asked why on earth I was licking her heels like that.

'You were so seductive, Squirrel. I let myself go. But I didn't really want it.'

'And why not? After all, we sleep in one bed, we are a man and a woman, that could include a child.'

'Yes and no. You want a child, I feel pushed into a corner. As if I have no say in it. My mother made her decisions like that. For me it feels like a fait accompli. Do you understand that?'

She gave me a guilty look, but said: 'Jacob, I'm thirty-eight. If I wait any longer, I'll go crazy. I need a child! That's my nature.'

Defeated, I kissed her amicably on the cheek, realizing

that the looming presence of 'our' child was still months away. Besides, I could not imagine that a conception would have taken place. Hundreds of years ago, yes, but whether my seed was still viable in the present? I very much doubted that. So, I shrugged it off. Nothing to worry about yet.

Sam, relieved by my apparent acceptance, became pleasant company again. We went into a tapas bar and refreshed ourselves with cold beers and tasty snacks.

'Do you know where the word tapa comes from?' Sam leafed through a tourist brochure.

'No, tell me.'

'In the old days, people put a slice of bread on their wine glass to protect it from flies. Then some bartender put a slice of ham or cheese on the bread, and that's how the tapa was born.'

'Then why is it called tapas?'

'Ah si, tapa means cover or lid.'

Boabdil's story

The next days, we visited like real tourists the Arab cultural heritage of Seville. We strolled through the alleys and delved into the city, which was very crowded and noisy as well. Yet strangely enough, even in the Alcazar, where the Arab influence was so evident, I had no urge to take the sage.

On our second day in Seville, Sam suddenly got tired of eating in restaurants. She suggested we buy some goodies and have a picnic in the park. In a small supermarket we bought cheese and ham, a can of sardines, fresh bread, olives, tomatoes, and a cucumber. I chose a bottle of rose, which was in a fridge. Between the fragrant flowers on surrounding bushes, we wandered through the gardens of the Alcazar and snuggled cross-legged across from each other in the shade of a majestic palm. Sam made sandwiches. I had to admit, I enjoyed the food. We had a good time, and after lunch and the cool wine, we stretched side by side in the thin grass, heads on our backpacks. For a while, I stared mindlessly at the silhouette of the palm against the blue sky and followed the sparrows picking up the breadcrumbs around us. Then I dozed off.

For at least an hour, I'd slept and felt recovered afterwards. I looked beside me and saw Sam's place empty. I got up and sat down on a bench in the shade. The past few days, I'd hardly read, I now saw my chance to enjoy my freedom for a while.

I pulled Washington Irving's *The Conquest of Granada* from my backpack. Irving, an American diplomat in the nineteenth century, chronicled Spanish life, while travelling. *The Conquest of Granada* was set in the last twenty years of the fifteenth century in the Caliphate of Granada. Irving described every battle in great detail, one could imagine, he was actually present at the time, as it seemed he had known all characters personally. This book was scientifically deemed worthless and scornfully dismissed as too romantic. Still, I read some passages with fascination. Somewhere, my eye fell on the name 'Morayma' and I was immediately alert.

'Ali Atar, Morayma's father, was a seasoned warlord and a ruthless enemy of the Christians. His name was highly regarded by his officers. From his fortress, he followed every movement of the Christian army, as soon as he saw the shimmering flower of Spanish Christian knighthood preparing for battle, he exclaimed excitedly and confidently: 'Thanks for the help of Allah. I'll teach those arrogant horsemen of Ferdinand a lesson.'

He invested his entire private fortune in the army to defend his city of Loja. By the time his daughter married Boabdil, there was no money left for the wedding dress and the bride had to borrow her dress and jewelry.

Ferdinand had become so optimistic after his first major victory over Alhama de Granada in 1482, he thought his next target, Loja, was easily conquered. The city was strategically situated between Cordoba and Granada and Ferdinand must have thought, Loja would be a clever springboard to Granada.

But the king had not reckoned with the crafty warriors of Ali Atar, the lord and master of the Loja region, who knew every bush and rock. Ferdinand miserably lost the battle and with it, many men. He fled and drifted to Cordoba to consider a new tactic.

I grew bored with the richly colored descriptions Washington Irving presented to me, and the heavy book sank into my lap. I dozed off in the sultry silence of the garden and imagined myself on a bench in the garden of the Alhambra and recalled Boabdil. I had experienced the man at different stages in his life, which had connected me with him so much, I almost felt like his alter ego. Enthralled, I listened to that voice with a faint echo from a distant past: 'Unrest, rebellions and uncertainty buzzed through the city.

The Christians were everywhere. They were gaining more and more influence. My father, Muley Hacen had a lot of power, people were afraid of him, he sowed division and set up our own people, the Muslims, against each other. He had a lot of influence among the wealthy families who no longer cared about their faith, some had married into Catholic families. However, the wealthy rulers of Granada, the Abencerrajes, were loyal to me and my mother and our Islamic faith. They helped us to dethrone my father.

Until father changed his strategy. He pretended to retire and made me think I was firmly in control, so I married Morayma. After our first meeting I had seen her twice more and both times had been very touching and intimate. The wedding lasted four days and our happiness would last a lifetime, we were convinced of that. We sang, danced, and ate in the gardens of the Alhambra, together with hundreds of guests. Even my mother behaved herself. My young wife was delighted with my exclusive gifts, especially the black diamond. The ancient gemstone that came from none other than Allah. This stone represented the power of the Nasrid family and was passed down from generation to generation. For Morayma, the diamond sealed our loyalty, she thought she would become the most beautiful and richest sultana of Granada.

That's what I wanted to believe too; we were happy and in love. But two days later I had to leave for a battle. My steel surcoats were richly decorated and studded with gold nails. They had been polished and rubbed and I had a beautifully crafted helmet on my head. One of my men sheathed a sword and dagger on my belt. They were sharper than sharp. I was handed a round shield with the Nasrid coat of arms and a long lance. I was well armed and well prepared; nothing could go wrong.

But on leaving the Alhambra through the Elvira gate I thrust my lance and the point broke. The soldiers in my immediate vicinity saw it happen and were shocked.

'This is a bad omen, master,' whispered Ahmed, my most loyal servant. Of course, I pretended nothing was wrong. I refused another lance and unsheathed my sword. I resolutely rode forward, leading my men out of town, hiding my fear and lack of experience behind my bravado, because deep in my heart I also believed in this bad omen.

First, we went with our small army through the country, to quell uprisings among our own people and to show Ferdinand our teeth. Sometimes, I could go home for a night and sleep in my young wife's arms. Our first son would soon be born, and the knowledge that I would not be present at his birth tore Morayma apart. She cried a lot, sometimes all night. The next morning, I left her, with a heavy heart. I had to re-join with my men. Under my father-in law's inspiring leadership, our army grew. Perhaps we were overconfident, because at one point my army numbered ten thousand soldiers and we rode with twelve to fifteen hundred horses. And this was exactly what my father had orchestrated.'

Confrontation

'Jacob, Jacob!' A scream drove Boabdil's voice from my head. Blinking in the light, I forced myself to abandon my daydream.

'Oh, you're still here?' Sam came briskly to me, as if she was a galloping horse. 'Come on, dude, I met a nice Irish couple. We will meet them on a terrace for a drink.'

Now, with my eyes wide open, I looked at my girlfriend. Her tanned face had more freckles than ever, she stood in front of me and laughed with big yellow teeth. She pulled the clip from her thick hair held it between her teeth, as if it was a bit and shook her hair loose. She took the hair off her shoulders again, twisted it together on top of her head, and fastened it again with the clip. My eyes caressed her beautiful long neck that shone like that of a thoroughbred mare.

Fully aware of myself sitting next to Boabdil, I saw a horse in Sam. I staggered to my feet, but slumped back onto the bench and inhaled the strong smell of something sweet. A few green parakeets chattered above me in a tree. Strange, how only now I noticed them. My senses were so tense. Was it all one big daydream, or reality? I realised I was moving between two worlds again. I now had to enter Sam's world, I had to leave that other one, which mainly took place in my head, behind my eyes. She pulled me to my feet and lashed onto me as if I were her mount that she'd saddled.

Slowly, I came back to reality. Her reality, not mine. Goddammit, what was she talking about? Socialising with some couple was the last thing I felt like doing.

But I no longer had a choice. A little later, I sat on a busy terrace under a green umbrella behind a large glass of beer, listening to the conversation between Sam and one very blond Isa. Her husband, Fred, tried to start a conversation with me, but I couldn't concentrate on his questions. I considered their names. Was it a coincidence that her name was Isa? Isabella, and his was Ferdinand? Too bizarre. My conversation with Boabdil was still fresh and I now sat with this couple of disguised Catholic kings.

'Sam told me you are engrossed in the history of Andalusia,' I heard him say.

'Ah, she told you that?'

'It's your job, isn't it?'

'Yeah, uh, what's your name again?'

'Fred, I just told you.'

'No, I was thinking of your real name, could it be Ferdinand?'

'No, Frederick.'

'Oh, well I think Ferdinand sounds better, you know. You have something like a proud monarch.'

The man laughed heartily and took my rudeness for a good joke, but that was not what I wanted at all. I was looking for a fight, to get off that terrace as soon as possible.

'And your wife is like the queen, Isabella.'

She looked up and said: 'Indeed, that's my name, but I like Isa, it sounds nice.'

'You think so?' I sneered.

Unaffected, Fred said: 'I've read also about the Arabs and the Catholic kings, you know.'

'Did you?' I didn't want to talk about that, not with this

guy with his red burnt face, and sunglasses over his eyes, in which I saw myself. But the damage was already done. Fred began to preach in Richards' teaching tone, the obnoxious university professor, who always sought confrontation and woe with you if you didn't agree with him. I, a twenty-year-old stubborn student, opposed the man bravely. Richards beat me all the time, though I didn't admit that, of course. I lost the battle and never apologised. Neither did he, by the way.

'Great kings, they were.' Fred's voice pulled me out of the memory. 'Especially she, but he also. Ferdinand was a brave ruler with a great vision, who tolerated his wife next to him.'

I had scarcely delved into the background of Los Reyes Catholicos and meekly listened.

'Maybe he had to because she was so dominant? Sam suggested.

'Maybe.' Fred smiled at her forgivably. 'They were cousins, you know. He was heir to the throne of Aragon and she of Castile. With their marriage the empire was doubled. Isabella's half-brother and king, Henry IV, was vehemently against the marriage because they were related. Officially they had to ask permission from the Pope, which Isabella refused. Henry had his half-sister closely guarded, but still, she secretly prepared their marriage. He closed all borders with Aragon to prevent Ferdinand from traveling to his future consort. However, the couple were not to be fooled.' Fred looked around triumphantly, took a gulp of beer and continued: 'Disguised as a mule driver, he arrived in Castile after having defied all dangers. Then and there, he nearly lost his life. A zealous city guard sneered at the mule driver and threw stones at him. In the end, the couple managed to marry with a forged papal marriage license.'

'Nice Fred, such details. Jacob never tells me things like that.'

I looked at Sam in surprise; what a nasty remark. 'Nothing but legends,' I muttered. 'Romantic love stories have always been your favorites.'

'No Jacob,' Sam cried, 'you know what I mean.'

'Oh, we have this too,' said Isa. 'I am an economist at the Ministry of Finance, do you think Fred is interested in my work, not at all.' She smiled and patted Fred on the arm. Rather patronising, I thought, but he didn't seem to mind.

I tried to swallow my irritation. I knew I was wrong but couldn't admit it. I felt like a spoiled kid who didn't get his way. That sentimental sense of loneliness overcame me again, that feeling of 'being excluded', I knew so well from boarding school. Why was that? Sam was right of course. I didn't try very hard to get her interested in my world. Was I the selfish bastard, she sometimes called me?

Fred was okay, of course, but I didn't give him a chance. He was more verbal than I, and he had lots to say too. Perhaps I could tell him about the sage and my lonely trips to the past. I would love to have a confidant. Not Angel, someone else, someone more educated. Maybe he would want to have a "trip" together with me.

'Do you know anything about Moorish history, Fred?' I asked, more leniently.

'Hardly anything. My interest is Catholicism. I'm not interested in Islam.'

'What? How can you say that? Islam is the cradle of our

culture. With its disappearance, Spain collapsed completely in the sixteenth century.'

'How do you mean? The Spaniards discovered South America and that's when it all started.'

'By stealing all that Inca gold, for sure. Do you know we owe our present civilization to the seven centuries of Islamic refinement? Our language, poetry, arithmetic, architecture, music, you name it, we owe everything to them. I would be proud if I was a Muslim.'

'Ah, Jacob, aren't you exaggerating? They may have contributed, but like the Romans, they have succumbed to their own decadence.'

Fred's plain arrogance turned me on. The same unreasonable rage as a few days ago, - when Sam had told me so bluntly, in her sweetest voice, that she might be pregnant, - bubbled up. Then, I had managed to curb the beast that erupted in me. Now, I couldn't anymore.

Furiously I jumped up. My chair tipped backwards, the beer glasses on the rickety table toppled, and I sauntered off, through the crowd. The stunned looks of Sam and her new friends following me.

This was not how I knew myself. I never got so angry, I used to be phlegmatic, even in my classes I let the students walk over me. Was I tainted by reading about those battles and warlords who smashed in each other's heads? Or was something wrong with my metabolism that caused these mood swings?

Sam ran after me. 'Jacob, what's the matter with you? Don't be childish.' She grabbed my arm and pulled me to a stop.

'I will no longer be insulted.'

'But he didn't insult you at all.'

'What do you know about that?'

'You are overreacting.'

'You know what, you go out with them. Eat with them, have a good time. You people are a good match. I'm of a different breed.'

'Oh, Jacob, please.' She squeezed my arm viciously.

'Ah, Sam, please,' I chided after her. When I saw tears glistening in her eyes, I jerked free and ran off.

While her uncomprehending, tearful look dancing behind me, I coincidentally found our hotel, nearby.

'Ha,' I said out loud, kicking my sandals into the corner and dropped onto the bed. 'Ma'am has lost power over me once again. I would now choose for myself. Long-time-no see, friend. I'm back where I belong.'

Santa Fe

*T*he air conditioner blew stale air into the room and the thermometer told me it was 36 degrees, outside it was something like 45 degrees. Good, great difference, I sighed. I took out my diary and leafed without energy through it. I always used to like to make notes, I needed to catch up with the days in Loja and Seville, but I lacked the will to write.

I picked up the top book from the stack next to the bed, opened it and started reading. Alhama de Granada, 1482. That battle was the beginning of the end for Al-Andalus. I wanted to know the details but couldn't concentrate and I shut my eyes. Even before I fell languidly into a half-sleep, the book slipped from my hands. I just sensed Boabdil beside me on the edge of the bed. He had grown old and was thoughtfully talking to me.

'It wasn't until the spring of 1491, that I saw clearly how I stood with my back against the wall. I had no choice, but to surrender Granada, to spare as many of my fellow believers as possible.' He poked his cane at an imaginary dust ball between his feet. 'My father had died in 1485. His brother, my uncle Al Zagal, who replaced me during my captivity, fled Almería after my liberation and left for Morocco with his total entourage. All responsibility for the Caliphate of Granada, actually only the city was left, was on me.'

'You then got in touch with Ferdinand, and want to work with him?' I asked timidly, interrupting his story seemed completely inappropriate, but I wanted to make contact, and see how real he was.

He straightened and poked the floor even more emphatically, the iron point tapping the tiles. 'Ferdinand was in charge of the Inquisition, and foreign affairs. It was Isabella who took care of the preparations for the Conquest of Granada, and she did so with incredible precision. New artillery, the latest inventions of weaponry from France and Italy, ammunition from Flanders, the best doctors; she took her time, and forgot nothing with her boundless talent for organizing. She definitely was a personality. Capable and powerful. Not a woman to be trifled with.'

Fascinated by his candor, I sat up straighter and listened attentively to Boabdil. For a while he stared at my wobbly hammertoes. I forced myself to keep quiet, not wanting to distract him.

'I had realised how important it is to put oneself in the position of someone else. I had learned to listen. Not to bring my own views to the front. You know... .' Boabdil thoughtfully spoke to himself. 'War is fueled by megalomania and need for power. Two camps are created. There is no unity, only difference.' He paused. It took a long time, and I wondered if he would ever start talking again.

Suddenly he continued in a different tone: 'For a few weeks Morayma and I had been living in the Alhambra again. I sat in the gardens, meditating and contemplating my chances. My dearly beloved wife approached me, closely followed by Gonsalvo Hernandez de Cordoba, Isabella's right-hand man. I knew Gonsalvo, and his older brother, Alfonso de Aquilar, quite well. They were orphans as kids. We used to play together; we were blood friends. He brought me a letter from the king with the order to surrender Granada immediately.'

'Your old friend came with a capitulation order?' I asked.

'Shh,' Boabdil raised his hand. 'Of course, I knew my fate: further resistance was futile and cause for more bloodshed. However... ' For the first time Boabdil gave me a piercing look. 'My big ego got in the way; my self-esteem forbade me to capitulate. I wanted to defend the Alhambra until the day I died.'

'But you knew Isabella's army was powerful.'

'Yes, and at the time, I had no idea that her army was also so modern.'

'Gonsalvo was el gran Capitan, wasn't he?'

'Gonsalvo was el Gran Capitan!' Boabdil ran an outstretched

hand through his hair, ruled by grey locks. 'He'd worked his way up, from soldier to Isabella's first general. You know, my childhood was dominated by betrayal between my parents and my family. In his youth there was not much parental love either, which created a bond between us, and I so badly wanted to trust him. But he benefited from the intrigues and owed his success to the prevailing war climate. Though, I must admit, he had many brilliant qualities. Gonsalvo used to be a nice guy. Well-educated, he spoke Arabic, was sporty and a brave fighter with great strategic and diplomatic perception. When I saw Gonsalvo again after all these years, I immediately knew that he still respected me. A general of his caliber would not rise again soon.'

'He was considered Isabella's crown prince,' I said.

Boabdil nodded. 'The Catholics had built their army camp outside Granada, with a beautiful view over the Vega. Isabella was often there and knew how to get her soldiers excited. She visited the quarters every day and was proud of her field hospital with doctors from abroad, who treated wounded soldiers as quickly as possible.'

'One time, Isabella wanted to take a trip into town,' I told Boabdil, hoping I could keep the dialogue going. 'A small delegation, led by Gonsalvo, got no further than La Zubia. The Muslim villagers were amazed to encounter such a small Catholic army unit and attacked. The royal delegation bravely fought back. An eyewitness later reported that the entire population of the village had been staring open-mouthed at Isabella. She fought like a man.'

Boabdil chuckled, tapping his stick on the pile of books beside the bed. 'This knowledge is in here?'

I nodded.

'I didn't know that. I'm dead, but still alive in books?'

'You live on in me.' I wondered if I was going crazy, but no one needed to know about this conversation. Whether it was in my mind or in real life, it was important to me.

'Isabella's tent caught fire one night in July,' the sultan said. 'Some of the tents around hers also went up in flames.' He got up and paced the room around the bed. 'Her entire wardrobe was lost. Gonsalvo, practical and polite as he was, made sure the Queen had a new wardrobe the next day.'

'How did he get it there so quickly?' I hadn't read this anecdote anywhere before.

'He had his own wife's entire wardrobe delivered. Isabella was amazed by the beauty of her clothes.' He laughed briefly. 'She had not expected such exquisite clothes from a civilian woman. In any case, the fire was a reason to look for better housing for the soldiers.'

Through the half-open bathroom door, I saw him examining himself in front of the weathered mirror above the sink. I heard him pee.

'She had all the houses evacuated in the nearest town. There was enough room for the various legions. She named the village Santa Fe. It was the first place with a Christian name in the province of Granada.' Back in the room, he sat down on my bed again. 'Gonsalvo and I rekindled our friendship. I appreciated his company, and we had some fruitful discussions. I trusted him, my blood brother, and that's where I went wrong. He undermined my authority. He had spies everywhere and bribed my most loyal people with oriental gifts. His knowledge of Arabic and my friendship made him like one of us, which gave him a lot of credit from my people.'

I woke up to the sound of the toilet flushing, the light was on. Sam stamped across the room and crawled under the sheet next to me. She didn't give me a glance. I smelled the alcohol on her breath. She fell asleep like a log. On her watch I saw it was almost twelve o'clock.

I flipped on the bedside lamp on my side, and picked up the book, fallen from my hands, hours earlier.

LUCENA

Captivity

I woke up before Sam, calling her loudly to arouse her. She moaned and stumbled into the shower. We had breakfast on a terrace. She kept her sunglasses on, although the sun had not yet come up over the city's rooftops. I chatted cheerfully about this and that, while she kept silent. Only after the second cup of coffee she mumbled, to my repeated question if she had a good time, 'Yes, it was fun.'

'Good for you, good food?'

'The full moon hung over the city like a creamy ball, it was magic.'

'And what were you all talking about?'

'Oh, about their work, my work.'

'About me too?'

'No, Jacob, not about you. But we've exchanged addresses, we'll keep in touch.'

'Typical. Nice for you.'

'You've behaved outrageously, I'm really annoyed.'

'They behaved outrageously.'

Sam sighed theatrically. She looked at me over the rim of her sunglasses, shaking her head, refraining from any further comment.

After a while she said: 'I've seen enough of Seville. I would like to go to Portugal and enjoy a nice beach on the Algarve.'

'Portugal?'

'Fred and Isa gave me some nice addresses.'

Of course, that lazy bunch. 'No way. We are going to Cordoba, according to our plans. We can't miss that. Do you know how special the Mezquita is?'

'I'm sick and tired of your history madness.'

'I'm not.'

After her return last night, I couldn't sleep with the noise of her snoring. I hoped Boabdil would come back, he still had to finish his story, but I had lost contact. I read in another book about those early times, ten or twelve centuries ago: the Arabs had settled in Cordoba and built Medina-al-Zahara. A modern city with avenues, palm trees, palaces, bathhouses, and mosques. Many Jews lived in Cordoba as well at the time, and together they, Muslims and Jews, took the culture to unprecedented heights.

Unfortunately, within a century, the Berbers destroyed the place again. I orated to Sam, as if she was a student in my class: 'In the tenth and eleventh century, the construction of the great mosque began, a masterpiece with refined, sober architecture. In the sixteenth century, the Christians built a Catholic cathedral in it, words such as bombastic and pompous would fit. We wouldn't want to miss this phenomenon.'

Sam pressed her sunglasses more firmly on her nose and yawned. She ate her toast, took a sip of coffee, and didn't seem to resist me. So much the better, I planned to take another trip to the past in the mosque. Gradually, I even was beginning to long for it again. There was still enough sage of the ghosts to experience the whole Moorish history. We had another week of holiday, and now she wanted to go to Portugal? No way! As long as we were in Andalusia, my traveling back in time would not be over.

Suddenly a feeling of panic overcame me. What would life be worth without the sage? The contents of that little box were the foundation of my life now. Not our house in Hackney or the students, I soon had to face again as a good-natured history teacher. My daily routine: cycling to school, a chat in the teacher's room, teenagers with bored faces, and my enthusiasm trying to motivate them, the weak cup of coffee from the machine during the break, and their homework I had to revise over the weekends, I couldn't do it anymore. Mind you, and then the other calamity lurked around the corner of my conscience. A baby, only a few molecules big, would change my entire life. I didn't want to think about my life, neither past, nor future. Suddenly, I knew for sure: I wouldn't go back at all. I now had another life that held me in its grip.

Despite her pounding headache, Sam wanted to drive.

'Fine, then I'll read the map.'

'That's not necessary at all, because the highway to Cordoba is well posted.'

'Couldn't we take the country roads, then we'll see more of the interior landscape.' I spread the map on the hood and pointed out a route. My eye fell on Lucena, about 40 miles southeast of Cordoba. Not really on the route, but I suddenly got an uncontrollable urge to go there. This was the place where Boabdil was imprisoned in 1483.

I quickly folded the map and guided her behind the wheel. She followed my directions, not realizing we were not heading north, but back east. By the time we were supposed to be in Cordoba, she saw the sign: Lucena!

'Hey, is this right, Jacob? We have not seen one single sign to Cordoba. Man, where's your head?'

'Lucena?' I acted, 'how is that possible? Gosh Sam, how stupid of me. I don't know what came over me.'

Sam pushed her sunglasses down and looked at me with eyes crackling like electric sparks. 'I don't like this at all, man.'

'Sorry Squirrel, my fault. Let's have a drink here and some lunch. It doesn't matter, it was a beautiful drive, wasn't it?' I pointed to a parking lot under some trees, and we got out. As soon as we sat on the terrace of a restaurant, with a few tables occupied by Spaniards, a girl came out to take our order.

'Tell me what's so exciting about this place,' Sam asked benevolently.

'Okay, I read about it last night,' I began cautiously. 'In the early eleventh century this was mainly a Jewish community in Islamic Al-Andalus. But in 1320 Lucena was conquered by the Catholics. In 1483, Boabdil came here with his army, commanded by his father-in-law Ali Atar, and unexpectedly stood face to face to the vast army of Ferdinand.'

Two beers were put on the tab, and I immediately took a big sip to lubricate my dry throat.

'At first the Arabs held out bravely, but suddenly we were attacked from behind by a small Christian army of about fifteen hundred men, which completely shattered us. Shocked, I heard rumors of Ali Atar's death, and suddenly, I had to take over the entire armed forces. There were several options to consider. We could fight on, which would mean... '

'Jacob, you are speaking in the first person. What's wrong with you?'

Startled, I looked at her. I hadn't noticed. 'Gosh, funny, uh, well, then it means uh, maybe more to you,' I stammered.

Sam tapped her finger on her forehead, saying: 'Go on, my King and hero.'

Careful, not to make the mistake again, I continued: 'Okay, where was I. They would be slaughtered in cold blood, so Boabdil trumpeted: "Run! Get yourself to safety and pass the Xenil River." Due to heavy rainfall, the water had overflowed its banks, and crossing the river was out of the question. The Arabs were trapped like rats. Boabdil had made the wrong decision. More than five thousand soldiers were killed or captured. Even Boabdil himself, nobody had recognised him as the king. The days of fighting had made me one of them. He was handcuffed, like an ordinary soldier.'

'Jacob, I must say, you're a great teacher. I wish I had lessons from you at school. You have the skill to make it very visual.'

'Thank you.' I pretended not to hear her cynical tone. 'The sultan was humiliated and imprisoned, here in Lucena's castle by this bunch of barbarian Christians. Moreover, he was again confronted with the power of his father, the old king, Muley Hacen. It had been part of his strategy to get rid of his son, by having him captured. His father failed to assist Boabdil in the battle of Lucena, instead he handed him over to the Christians. Aided by his brother, Al Zagal, Muley Hacen returned to the throne. They chased mother and my wife, Morayma ... '

- I heard my slip and recovered: - 'His mother and wife out of the Alhambra and placed them in the Carmen el Palacio Dar al-Horra in the Albaicín. In the summer of 1485, Ferdinand released Boabdil. Dad had just passed away, and despite our struggles, I was sorry I couldn't attend his funeral.'

'You're doing it again?' Sam was listening attentively now.

'What?'

'Identifying yourself with that man.'

'What do you mean, I wasn't at my father's funeral, because I was in jail.'

'Jacob, that has nothing to do with the story of these lousy Moors.'

'Sam, everything! There are so many similarities between Boabdil and me. I sometimes believe I am his reincarnation.'

'You are crazy. And I'm really starting to believe that. The last few days you haven' been yourself, you're acting strangely, and your behavior is rude.'

'Don't talk like that, Sam. Don't be so angry. Do you want

to hear the rest of the story?'

Sam twisted her mouth into a straight line. She squeezed her hands around the back of the chair, her knuckles turned white, but she kept her mouth shut.

'Boabdil had the confidence of his own people. Even Ferdinand, found him a more accommodating negotiator than his father. During his captivity there was too much tension in the Nasrid Empire, Ferdinand couldn't handle it. Suddenly, Boabdil's freedom was important for the peace and general order in Granada.'

The girl came to bring two sandwiches with pork fillet.

'Nice, lomo!' Sam, instantly distracted, greedily took a bite.

I pushed my plate towards her. I never liked pork much, but at that moment I decided to quit completely. I thought of Ramadan, and wondered if I would go as far as that too. Fasting for a month. In my class, a few boys strictly adhered to it. Somehow, it had always intrigued me.

'You know what was so mean?' I continued, unperturbed. 'Boabdil was released, but they made him pay a heavy price. He had to sign a peace treaty, that left him powerless to take any more action. But the worst part was that he had to give up his children, the youngest was still a toddler. He had to agree to their Christian upbringing. That must have been terrible for Morayma. She saw little of her husband and lived mostly with her mother-in-law, Aisha, who was a dominant and bitter woman.'

'Do you know what Fred said? At the time, Aisha and Isabella were actually in power. Two strong women standing nose to nose.'

'Interesting, yes.' I put my fingertips together, I hadn't

thought of that before. 'Aisha was like my mother,' I mused aloud.

Sam rolled her eyes.

'It was unbearable for Morayma. She had such a sad life. She had to choose between the freedom of her husband or the kidnapping of her children. Can you imagine that?'

'Horrible.' At once, Sam was all compassion. I read in her eyes, the thought of her own child, and heard her mumble: 'I would always protect my child from such rudeness.' Then, her attitude changed, she emptied her glass and said: 'I have to go to the bathroom, shall we leave?' She stood up and went inside.

Weird, that comment hurt, but I understood it. Of course, she would be better off without me as the father of her child. Boabdil and his sons were allowed to officially visit Morayma once a year. But the boys spoke a different language and it was difficult for her to communicate with them. I would be something like that: a father for the weekends, the holidays, a father who spoke a different language. I knew what that meant and inside me a voice screamed: No!

I saw the loneliness of those boys before me because I had experienced it myself. I knew what it felt like to have your world smashed to pieces with a sledgehammer. My first holiday. I came home to Israel from boarding school in Italy. I longed for my father and mother but noticed their relationship had changed profoundly. Dad was clearly annoyed by Inez's inflated happiness. I never knew the exact cause of their marriage failure, but my instincts told me: The reason was me. I shouldn't have been born.

Boabdil and Morayma did not have a bad marriage, but

Yusuf and Ahmed hardly knew their father. After his release from the dungeons in Lucena, he lived somewhere outside Granada, an outlaw, not allowed to be with his family. He was unable to act politically. At that time, he was nicknamed Al Zogoiby, which means in Arabic, 'the unlucky one'.

Sam came out of the restaurant and called: 'I've already paid, are you coming?'

Kittens

In a small street next to the restaurant were containers for waste; glass, plastic, paper and cardboard, they even took in clothes and shoes. Great, I was fed up with the smelly garbage bag in our car. I picked it up and threw it in a container. When my foot hit a cardboard box next to it, I heard a soft plaintive cry. I bent down and opened the flaps. A kitten staggered across the corpses of his brothers and sisters. His blind eyes blinked against the bright light. Startled, I closed the box. Should I call Sam? Take the kitty to a vet? Or just let it die like the others. Couldn't we take it with us? It was a beautiful, red like-a-tiger animal. Indecisively I opened the box again and stroked his thin spine, his back bulging sensitively. He even had the energy to blow against that strange-smelling hand. Sam honked behind me. I swallowed the grim fate this little animal had met. He was born and unwanted. He had to die right away. How meaningless his existence was. I sat on my haunches, felt the blood flowing to my calves, which began to sting significantly.

The door of the car slammed shut behind me. Sam's voice: 'What are you doing, Jacob? Do you have to poop?'

Her shadow fell over my hand stroking the kitten. Its blowing had turned into purring, as if he did that for the first time in his life.

'Jesus, how pathetic. Are you crying? Jacob, there's only one thing to do here. She grabbed the little tiger from under my hand and placed the animal protectively against her chest. She muttered something sweet that I didn't understand. The next moment she slammed its head hard against the rim of the container in one swift motion. I heard the crack. She re-arranged the stiff bodies of the brothers and sisters and pushed Tiger's still limp and warm body between them.

Gasping for breath, I watched. 'How could you be so mean?'

'This kitten has no future, Prick. Now, he is out of his misery.'

Confused, I got into the car.

'I'll go wash my hands.' She disappeared back into the restaurant.

Upset, I stared at the dashboard. Sam returned, and fanatically pulled the car into reverse and drove off. From Lucena, I didn't get to see one bit, except for a restaurant, the main street, and a box of dead kitties. My plan, to get to see El Moral, the castle where Boabdil had been imprisoned, completely failed. My secret desire to take some sage here, had gone up in smoke. The next hour we drove through a barren, mainly flat, landscape under the blistering Andalusian sky.

Looking at the endless rows of olive trees, I heard the snap of the cat's neck, like a repeating thump in my head.

The animals from my earliest childhood passed through my memories. Guy, my parakeet, who'd died of starvation. Inez cleaned his cage and found a vicious rat in his feeder. Harry hamster escaped when I cleaned his cage. He must have disappeared in the laundry basket, because days later Inez dredged his skeleton out of the filter of the washing machine. Joe, our cat, liked to curl up in the oven and died when Inez made apple pie. Kyra, the dachshund, got his tail between the door and bled to death. After losing him, I never wanted a pet again.

Sam put her right hand on my knee. 'Jacob, your leg is wet. Are you still mourning about that cat?'

I hadn't noticed. My throat was closed. Once, long ago I had animal friends that consoled me and I had no clue what happened to them. Did Inez bury them? Did we talk about it? Had I ever cried?

'Am I very soft?' I muttered aloud.

Sam squeezed my knee. 'A little, but no, this is a very painful memory, you felt in your childhood.'

I nodded.

'Do you want to talk about it?'

I appreciated she didn't laugh at me. I started to tell her about Guy, who pecked breadcrumbs off my lips and literally played soccer with a ping-pong ball. Harry, who always went round and round in his little mill. Joe, who purred on my lap and loved the heat so much, it killed him.

'You know,' I said, 'my father thought I should get tough.'

'Really? And what about Inez, wasn't she sensitive about those things?'

'I think so, but at the end of the day, they had no time for me.'

'What else do you remember?'

'Don't know. Maybe I have it all wrong, I have a certain idea of my upbringing. It was wrong, but it was mine, and I grew out of that. Maybe I just stigmatized my parents incorrectly.'

'No, I think you're very sensitive. And that is why it is important to have your own child, to be able to relive your own childhood.'

'Do you think so? I have mostly negative feelings for dad and maybe for Inez too. I don't want to go back to my youth anymore.'

Sam nodded; her voice became softer. 'Thanks for telling me this.' She added, after a brief silence: 'Parents do what is within their power. It makes no sense to blame them for their failures.'

'They acted without thinking about the consequences. Inez was so young when she married dad.'

'Exactly, you can't continue to blame her for her faults. I think you should talk to her. You both have different perceptions of the same thing.'

Sam was probably right. I just had to talk to Inez, and then out of the blue, I said: 'Maybe I'll want a cat when we get home. Or a dog.'

Without taking her eyes off the road, she said: 'We'll see, first have a baby.'

As if a floodgate had closed, holding back the swirling slurry. Sam used her whip and chased me back into my cage. Something had come loose, it was unstoppable, a tsunami of feelings, but she turned the tide. I bit my lip, tried to harden myself, be stoic, and I threw this dead tiger kitten behind the wall, together with all those other corpses from my youth. I had to start all over again. How could I have thought I was in touch with myself. No way. Only in the past with Boabdil, five centuries ago, could I allow such feelings. Then and there, I was allowed to be weak and cry. In this present, this chill modern and technological age, I walked around in an emotional chainmail suit. Boabdil's army could envy that. I grinned. That's how I knew myself again. I knew how to act tough.

CORDOBA

Medina al Zahara

We were approaching Cordoba. The silhouette of the city became visible. I knew the turnoff to the old city, Medina-al-Zahara, would show up soon, I sat straight and said: 'Why not visit Medina-al-Zahara, now.'

'That ruin? We're not going there,' Sam said sharply.

'No, no, we can go there tomorrow. too. Although, it's just three o'clock, what else could we do this afternoon?'

'Find a hotel, have a late lunch, I could do with a siesta, I still have a pounding headache. Tomorrow is another day.'

'Tomorrow we're going to the mosque.'

Behind her sunglasses, Sam's eyes widened with shock. 'Not all day, I hope?'

'Squirrel, listen. In this barren landscape in the year 800, water flowed through aqueducts, there were avenues with streetlights, palaces plastered with gold, alleys with palm trees. Let's go to that ruin now, just an hour. It's not that big.'

'Now? Is the hottest part of the day. You're crazy.'

'Okay, then let's eat first.'

'Damn Jacob, I don't like this. When are we going to do it my way?'

'Ninth century, tenth century, palm trees and oranges grew here in geometrical patterns. A city had been built here in only one century. There were universities, bathhouses, hundreds of shops, and perhaps a thousand mosques.'

'You don't listen to me at all.'

'Imagine, *One Thousand and One Nights*. Listen to this poem, I know it by heart: 'A palm tree stands in the middle of Rusafa, born in the west, far from the land of palms. I said to it: how like me you are, far away and in exile; In long separation from family and friends. You have sprung from soil in which you are a stranger; And I, like you, are far from home.'

Abd-al-Rahman-I, wrote this little tribute to the palm tree around 786. He knew he would never see his beloved homeland, Syria, again.'

'Jacob, I want to go to a hotel, lie down, and have a drink.'

'Didn't you drink enough last night?'

'Shit man, listen.'

'Precisely. Listen. Because that's what I wanted to tell your friend Fred yesterday. The Arabs had a tremendous lead, and although it has been their downfall, we are still living on it.'

'Okay.' Her eyes spat fire behind the brown glasses. 'We are going now! But I give you exactly one hour. One hour! After that we'll do what I want.' Sam braked vigorously, when a bright pink sign indicated the next turnoff to the ruins of the Medina-al-Zahara. The reason she obeyed me must have been my coercive attitude towards Fred, yesterday. Power tickled in my fingers, I didn't have to be the wimp who nodded yes and amen to what my girlfriend said, or what my mother thought? Her nasty comment to Fred that I didn't tell her about history was still fresh in my mind. Of course, I wanted to involve her in my world, but to what extent was she at all interested?

She parked the car and fished her hat off the backseat. Walking beside me to the more than a thousand-year-old ruin, she meekly asked: 'What about those Umayyads and Abassids?'

'Didn't I tell you that at the Alhambra?'

'Yes, but my memory is not as good as yours'.

I briefly repeated those details and continued: 'It was Abd Al Rahman-III, that is, the third descendant, who, in the middle of the tenth century, brought great wealth to the country, which at that time already included all of Al-Andalus. Christians, Jews, and Arabs co-existed peacefully. It wasn't until after 1009 that rival parties started clashing.' We walked past the excavations and foundations of what once were buildings.

'This place, Medina-al-Zahara, was then the Versailles of

Andalusia, one of the most acclaimed and architecturally interesting structures in the Islamic world. Built and destroyed within a century. Not by the Christians, but by the Muslims themselves.' I glanced sideways, at the shadow under her hat and quickly continued talking, before she could interrupt me. 'To keep the peace between the different tribes and caliphates, they called for the help of soldiers, the Berbers from the mountains of North Africa. However, they were uncivilized and unaccustomed to the culture prevailing here. As a result, the Muslim community became divided. There were at least sixty Taifa's, larger or smaller states, each with its own autonomy, populated by Berbers, Ummayads, old aristocratic Muslims and Jews. Jews were strongly represented at the time. They often had important functions and were active in the field of medicine and literature.'

'In which century are we now?' Sam asked.

'Eleventh, twelfth century. In the north of Al-Andalus, the Christian provinces woke up. They wanted to expand their territory and began to push their borders. Suddenly there were Muslims living in Christian cities. They were called Mudejar's, along with Arabized Jews and the Moss Arabs, or Arabized Christians. And then there were the Marranos, Jews who had become Christians. In the following years, Al-Andalus became a great melting pot of languages, religions, style, clothes, food, music, architecture. Everything was exchanged.'

'So, you could call that positive.'

'Yes. Each time, many decades passed, and they always found a balance.'

Sam looked at her watch: 'Okay, it's time. Jacob, I've seen

it here. I am dying of thirst; my headache is pounding like a church bell: The rest of the day is my decision.'

Stunned I stood still. I really thought she was interested and liked my lessons. So that's how far my power reached. It was exactly within the range of what she stated, what her deal was. One hour. Disappointed, I trudged after her, back to the car. Suddenly, she walked a lot more briskly, opened the car, tossed her hat into the backseat, slid behind the wheel, and set the airco on full blast. I was hardly settled into the seat next to her, when she tore out of the parking lot, with a tail of dust whirling behind us.

Cordoba lay vast and dreamy on the banks of the Guadalquivir River, which was almost dry. Rich fringes of pink oleander blossomed on the banks below the walls, and behind them rose the huge ochre edifice of the mosque.

Sam followed the signs to *centro ciudad*. We stopped at a traffic light, she said: 'I'm driving into that parking garage.'

Before I knew it, she braked for a yellow-and-black striped bar, pulled a card from the slot, stuck it between her teeth and drove into the gaping maw of an underground garage. Slowly, we circled down into the depths of the Earth's crust, where hundreds of cars stood patiently waiting in line for their drivers, till they needed them again. That oppressive darkness frightened me.

'Perfect.' Pleased with herself, Sam deftly parked into a narrow parking space. We left our stuff in the car and found the elevator that took us back to street level. At once, we were surrounded by crowds and the searing heat. Cordoba is a rather provincial town, smaller than Granada and Seville. I pointed to the Mezquita sign and started walking. In no time we were in the Judería, the Jewish quarter, where also several hotels were located.

Sam stopped at a terrace. 'Let's have a drink first. I'm dehydrated and in the mood for an ice-cold beer and tapas.'

'Helps to get rid of your hangover,' I sneered and kept walking.

'Who says I'm hungover?'

Right next to the mosque, overlooking the entrance, was a terrace. Sam sank into a chair made of plastic rattan and beckoned the waiter.

A busload of colorful tourists was being ushered into the mosque, and Sam said: 'I really don't need to see all those tourists in that mosque.'

Without responding to her easily achieved success, I said neutrally: 'I read somewhere that admission is free between eight and ten in the morning.'

'Okay, okay, eight o'clock tomorrow. We are here. Cameras ready.' To illustrate her tremendous enthusiasm, she waved a cheer through the air with her right arm.

'You don't have to come. I don't mind going alone.' I even preferred to go alone. As if she sensed that, she said, grinning triumphantly behind her golden beer: 'Prick, we're going together, and we'll have a good time.' She took a swig and added: 'The fact is, I don't trust you at all, and I've just decided that I won't let you out of my sight again.'

'We'll see.'

As long as the bottom of her beer glass was not in sight, we sat in silence, watching the pedestrians.

Opposite the mosque we took up residence in hostal El Triunfo. Sam stretched out on the bed and massaged her temples. 'Just a siesta first. We'll get our stuff later.'

I stared out of the window at the rough wall of the mosque. Should I lay down next to her? Or should I go straight into town now, alone? The constant ringing in my ears was debilitating, and the sharp images from that other time, which increasingly floated before my eyes like pop-ups from an Internet browser, weren't exactly liberating either. My eyes watered and burned. Yes, it would be better if I lay down next to her, for a while.

Hours later we woke up.

'God, it's hot in this room. Jacob, I think it's over forty-five degrees.'

I preferred to stay on the bed, still feeling exhausted, but Sam was already ambling around: 'Come on, let's go to the car, get our luggage, change clothes, and have dinner somewhere My stomach is roaring!

And back we walked, through the city to the garage, descended into the catacombs and moments later, like two real tourists, we pulled our rolling suitcases over the uneven pavement to the hotel.

I flipped through some folders, while Sam busily arranged her stuff, and took a brief shower. Instead of the shorts and the eternal T-shirt top, she suddenly walked in her new Zara dress. The afternoon nap and the prospect of food had clearly eliminated her headache. But now, I felt like a wreck, and had to pull myself together.

After nine, it was pleasantly busy in the Judería. The terraces were packed, but Sam found an empty table, in a corner. It still bothered me that she had abruptly cut me off in the ruins, but I wouldn't force my stories on her anymore.

There was plenty to see here and my attention was demanded by the surroundings. We sat in silence, like a couple who had nothing to say to each other after twenty years of marriage.

I took a gulp of wine and let it swish gently in my perpetually scorched mouth.

'Tell me more about Cordoba in the eleventh century,' Sam opened the conversation, to my surprise.

I uttered a sigh of relief. 'Okay, where was I again?'

'I don't know, tell me anything.' That sounded so uninterested again. Uncertainly, I began: 'The turnaround. In 1085 Alphons VI took possession of Toledo.' And as if the flames were rekindling under my smoldering enthusiasm, I continued: 'Alphons made Toledo the center of his Catholic kingdom and drove out or exterminated the Jews. He wanted to incorporate the southern, mainly Arab, provinces into his kingdom. This was opposed by the then Muslim ruler Muramid, who resided in Seville. Muramid enlisted the help of the Almoravids. These were fundamentalist Berber tribes, from Marrakech, who ruled over Morocco. They were fanatical and considered the Andalusians to be weak, because of their negotiating behavior with the Christians. They came as so-called protectors, but took over the country as tyrants, and Al-Andalus was increasingly ruled by foreigners, fanatic fighters from North Africa.'

Sam played absently with her napkin but listened. Even with a certain awe, I thought. From time to time, she looked at me intently and with admiration.

'The sophistication of the culture disappeared, but the Andalusians adapted. Around 1212 there was a second turning point. The Christians were now firmly in the saddle, led by Pope Innocent III. They defeated the weakened and divided Muslim cities of the south in succession. Cordoba fell in 1236, Valencia in 1238 and Seville became Christian in 1248.' I topped up our glasses and bit into a crust of bread. 'For the two hundred and fifty years that followed, the Caliphate of Granada survived, under the inspiring leadership of the Nasrids. They enforced a mandate over Granada, in exchange for military aid they gave at the battle of Cordoba. The Nasrids became the guardians of the memories of ancient Al-Andalus. Only then, the construction of the Alhambra began on the foundations of an old Jewish settlement.'

'So, the Muslims in Granada helped Cordoba into the hands of the Christians?' Sam interrupted. 'And they got away with the promise to handle their own business in Granada?'

I nodded vaguely and emptied my glass. My limbs were heavy, and my voice dragged, as if I was tipsy. From two glasses of wine? With my handkerchief I wiped the sweat from my forehead.

Sam patted my arm and gave me her sad puppy look. She said: 'Jacob, you are so different when you talk like this, so driven, so obsessed, it frightens me.' I had taken that look for admiration, but now I understood; she feared me.

Mezquita

*T*he next morning, we woke up around half past nine. Way too late. Sam first wanted breakfast, and she installed herself on a terrace bathing in early sunrays. I paced around her, indecisive, I would prefer to go into the mosque right now, as long as it wasn't too busy yet. However, my boss decided differently. And I didn't want trouble before the day had begun. To my surprise she dismissed me, with a wave of her hand. Go swinging, kid, her eyes seemed to say, Mama's coming to push you in a minute.

I crossed El patio de Naranjas, the open courtyard with rows of orange trees. On the pavement of round pebbles the tree trunks were planted inside round earthen holes connected by straight lines of water gutters. It was so quiet, it moved me and the atmosphere brought me back to Morayma, behind her spinning wheel.

In the mosque, I immediately got lost in a forest of red and white columns, an overwhelming repetition of pillars. I wandered around aimlessly. It was still quiet. A handful of curious tourists were taking pictures and a few guards stood indifferently at the entrances and exits. In awe, I felt absorbed by the infinity of the Muslim faith and was aware of Allah, watching over me.

I didn't know much about mosques, except that they were always built according to the same design. With the muezzin calling the believers from the minaret to prayer five times a day: 'Allah is great! On to prayer! To salvation! I bear witness, there is no other God but Allah and I bear witness, Muhammad is the messenger of God. God is big! There is no God but Allah alone!' I knew that on Friday all men are obliged to the great afternoon prayer. They must take off their shoes, so they do not desecrate the floor. In addition, they should ritually wash their hands, face and feet before taking up the holy book, the Quran. They pray facing Mecca. The direction is indicated by a niche in the wall, the so-called mihrab. This is the place from which the Imam, the pastor, utters the words of the Quran in which God reveals Himself.

I didn't notice anything yet about the presence of the Catholic cathedral. It was supposed to be here somewhere and thought, it wasn't all that bad after all, what those Catholics did in the sixteenth century.

The mosque was overwhelming, and I felt displaced. I began to long for the vacuum of that other time. I felt dizzy, and sweaty and hid behind a column. I tried to fantasise what it would be like to witness a prayer right now. How did people behave in the thirteenth century in Cordoba, when Muslims were still in the majority. My throat tightened at the thought of the Sage of the Ghosts. I got excited, just as that kid, I had seen rocking in Sam's eyes. Was she already inside? Walking around somewhere, or was she still sitting on the terrace? Maybe she was watching me. I looked around nervously but didn't see her anywhere.

I pulled the box from my backpack. I smelled the brown substance, the means of my transport. Once again it amazed me, how odorless the sage was. I broke off a little piece. As big as a blueberry. Not too much, I thought.

Before, I'd had been sitting when I took a bite, now I stood with my back to the pillar. My ears started to ring immediately. My tongue felt more burned than before, but it was also nice and intense. It seemed ages since I had experienced that sensation of tasting the sage. I counted quickly on my fingers; six days, that night in Loja had been the last time.

Not much happened. Was I already weaned from the stuff, and would each time take longer before something changed?

I moved away to a darker corner behind the columns. The buzzing in my head was now deafening. I put my palms against my temples. My head nearly burst, it felt like an anvil in a forgery, being beaten red hot. With my head between my hands, I blinked a few times. Dust swirled like gold powder in the streaks of light that poured into the building from somewhere. Workmen were busy here and there. Further on, I heard the chiseling on stone. Someone yelled. A squeaky chain hoisted chunks of stone past an unoiled pulley. Through the haze of swirling dust, I stared at the men, bare-chested in leather aprons. I was in the middle of the mosque where the forest of red and white columns was interrupted. A clearing in the woods. New trees were planted: slender, narrow pillars, more like the decoration on a cream cake. This had nothing to do with the sturdy, austere pillars of the mosque. There was activity everywhere, next to me, in front of me, and above my head. I looked around open-mouthed and didn't believe what I saw. A cathedral was built here, an imposing Catholic church, in the shape of a large cross.

In a daze I realised I was back in the sixteenth century. Didn't I take enough? I walked around carefully, as soon as

I touched anything, the spell would break, I knew that. In the pulpit a few men were putting up decorations in gold leaf and I let my finger hover at least an inch above the gold line of a groove in a column. From an unexpected corner I heard a scream. In a reflex I looked up and saw a huge chunk of marble topple from a column above my head. If I didn't jump, it would fall right on top of me. But I stood still. I couldn't move, my feet were glued to the ground. The block was going to fall now, but I couldn't jump.

'Jacob, Jacob!' That name echoed off the walls of the volcanic crater I was in. The boulder shattered beside me. The next moment, in a cloud of dust the men in leather aprons passed me in their shorts. Their bare torsos turned out to be T-shirts. The stones they carried were backpacks. Sam's face broke free from the clump of staring people around me.

'Jacob, what are you doing? You can't go there at all, man. You are on top of the pulpit.'

Then I collapsed. Both my worlds, my real and my fake, I didn't know which one I was in, whirled around me. In my mind, I sat on a stage behind closed velvet curtains. The audience was waiting for my performance, while I simmered between the folds and softness of a black nothingness. This was death. This is how death felt, I realised. Suddenly, the curtains opened.

Sam's face danced before my eyes. The tip of her ponytail tickled my chin. She slapped my cheeks, pulled the skin around my eyes, lifted the lids with her thumb, gave me a piercing look. She tried to drag me up, someone aided her. I couldn't help but cooperate. I wasn't dead after all. Slowly, I stepped back into the decor of my fake life.

The backpack

I lay flat in a bed, the frays of sleep slowly left me. My consciousness rolled back and forth like the rushing surf that rose up the beach at high tide and sank back to the sea with ebb.

'Jacob, wake up.' Sam shook my shoulder. 'You've slept for hours.'

Through my eyelashes I saw a plate of food in her hands. I was thirsty, unbelievably thirsty, but couldn't think about food.

My mind wandered to the mosque. I jolted awake when I thought of my backpack. Shit, did I leave that in the mosque? Behind that one distant column. My eyes drifted around the room, looking for my ancient, trusty backpack. Inez had given it to me when I turned sixteen. I would go camping in Dartmoor with a few friends. There, we smoked our first joints and for the rest of my life, I kept my weed crumbs and grams of hash in the secret inner pocket, behind an iron zipper. The space, where I now kept the box with Angel's herbal paste in.

'Sam, have you seen my backpack?'

'Great, you're back on Earth. Here's some food and water.'

'My backpack. Where is it?'

'I found it behind some column. That's very un-Jacob, I thought. You never lose sight of that tatty thing. So then, I went looking for you.'

'Give it to me!'

She handed me the limp grey rag. In her hands, my precious rucksack with its worn leather handles lost all its merit, while on my back it definitely had personality. I reached inside and felt the box in the inner pocket. Fortunately, she hadn't found that.

'We're going home,' Sam said. 'You are not well at all, you have bags under your eyes. You passed out in a place where no people are allowed. You've been acting strange, absent-minded and looking for a fight for days. Jacob, you are not yourself.'

'There's nothing wrong with me, Squirrel. But I'm on to something. Something very special.'

'What then? Why don't you tell me about it?'

'No, I can't. Later maybe when I am more sure.'

'What nonsense, such secrecy, as if I didn't notice anything?'

'It's much bigger than I am. It is bigger than our world, it spans many centuries. There is no past, present or future anymore. Everything that lives is connected through the ages. There is no death, or rather, everything is dead.' As I said those words, she looked down at me with that same puppy gaze as last night. Admiring, I thought then. Now I recognised it, in spite of my blurred vision, it contained compassion; she looked horrified.

'Jacob, your whole tongue is black.'

'Black?' I stuck my tongue out and forced my gaze down. The movement tired me, my tongue felt paralyzed. Speaking had taken some effort the past few days, but I could think just fine, and all the events in my mind were clear as glass. Yesterday, after I told the story, starting in the ruins of the medina and ending on the terrace in the Jewish quarter, my tongue felt like a dead animal hiding in my mouth. To be honest, I observed, that I had had this feeling already for several days.

Sam took a pocket mirror from her bag and held it up to my mouth. I took it from her hand, stuck out my tongue again and studied it. 'Black? Sam, you're exaggerating,' I said with difficulty. 'It's a bit colored like I've eaten liquorice.'

She snatched the mirror from my hand, exclaiming: 'That tongue is pitch black. Do you take something to live those great experiences of yours?' She didn't wait for my answer. 'My decision is made. We are going home. Besides, I don't have a moment of peace in my body, knowing I might be pregnant.'

Shit, that too, and I moaned: 'The wish is the father of the thought.'

'What? Yes, you are the father. Oh Jacob, I hope it worked. I can't wait to get my hands on a pregnancy test. Or shall I buy one here?'

I bit into the pillow and said nothing more. From now on, all my words would be misinterpreted. My sweet, free-spirited girlfriend was already almost a mother and from now on, all her conversations would be about names, diapers, and baby food. One day, Dr. Spock would be shoved right under my nose. My life was over. Sam sauntered to the bathroom. And I watched to this disastrous future played out in my mind's eye.

MADRID

The airport

The next morning, we left after breakfast for Madrid. Sam wanted to be on a flight to London that night, I wanted anything but that. She had it all arranged. I kept my mouth and behaved like a meek lamb. Sam chatted endlessly about nothing, but was at least cheerful, happy to go home. While I felt the opposite. God, how quickly lovers could grow apart.

'Toledo,' I read aloud. 'Can't we visit the city briefly? Take a walk through the Jewish quarter, eat something?' I tried.

'No way, I want to move on, otherwise we will be too late to book a plane tonight.'

'Well, then we're going tomorrow, why the rush?'

'No, I want to be in my own bed tonight, and see my doctor tomorrow.'

'Well, I don't. Jesus, Sam, I thought you were a bit more adventurous. We still have another week of holiday.'

'Not me. I'm sick and tired of this country, the heat, the food, all the driving.'

I stared out of the window. The fire was smoldering, and every word would catch a flame. After a while I said: 'It's already two o'clock, aren't you hungry, Squirrel?'

She half turned around and reached behind her, for her bag. The car swayed precariously. An Alfa Romeo was just overtaking us, honked alarmingly, and barely managed to avoid our car.

'Damn it, keep your hands on the wheel,' I screamed, my heart racing in my throat. 'I'll get that bag. Why actually?'

'I made sandwiches during breakfast, so we don't have to stop for lunch. I want one, do you?' She acted as if nothing had happened.

'No,' I hissed. But I did take a cheese sandwich from a napkin and gave it to her.

More than an hour later, we drove into the Avis parking lot. She handled the car rental. I fetched a cart for our luggage and trudged into the airport, after her. My shoulders drooped, my stride slow. Soon, all my courage, energy and passion for life would be left behind in the country, where I desperately wanted to stay. This time, my mind was not going to leave my body, but my body was going to leave my mind.

Sam headed for the Iberia counter.

'Uh, let's see.' The ground stewardess stared at the screen. 'Yes, there is another flight to London Heathrow at seven. Two seats?'

Sam handed over her credit card and a moment later, waved the tickets in front of my eyes. 'Four more hours! What are we going to do all this time?' I whined.

'Nothing. Look around and enjoy the coolness of the air conditioning.'

What a waste of time, how worthless. I slumped into the cushions of a lounge corner and grabbed a book from my backpack. There were still so many gaps in my knowledge, in particular Morayma, I had learned very little about her. Except that she married Boabdil when she was fifteen; that she languished in solitude, because Boabdil was mostly in prison; she suffered under her dominant mother-in-law; and that, in order to get her husband out of prison, she had to relinquish her children to the Catholic Monarchs, who insisted they receive a Christian education. Besides two sons, there was a little daughter, Aisha, who seemed to be Ferdinand's special toy.

With my eyes closed, I shut myself off from the buzz at the airport. After a while I heard Boabdil's voice again, as if it were my own.

'Ferdinand gave me my freedom back for the ransom of our two sons, Yusuf and Ahmed. There after Morayma was never the same; living without her children was too much of a burden on her young, fragile shoulders.' He sighed. 'I will never forget the day the letter came.'

'Letter?' I asked. What time was I in, the airport seemed so passionless to me.

'The letter was written on paper belonging to the Spanish court of Los Reyes Catholicos. I recognized the seal imprinted on the paper all too well, but the letter was written in our eldest son's untrained script. He thanked His Royal Highness for his sincere care, regretting his father, meaning me, would not return the honor and friendship to our great king.'

'That letter was dictated, of course!' I exclaimed indignantly.

A man in an office suit sitting across from me, looked at me over the edge of his laptop.

The sultan nodded. 'We were in the Carmen where Morayma and my mother were kept in exile. Morayma was in tears, and I couldn't stay. Again, I had to leave her in my mother's cold care.'

'Jacob, are you talking out loud?' Sam stood behind me, watching me closely.

Boabdil's voice sounded in my ears: 'Morayma regularly visited the astrologer Ben-Maj Kulmut, who had said: "The stars tell me that the last sultan of the Nasrids has suffered much in his long life." I could have told her that myself.'

I looked at Sam without seeing her properly.

Boabdil said: 'For Morayma those words were yet another reason to weep continuously, for it meant that she too had endured much grief in her short life. My poor sultana. She lived in my shadow without the love of her children and in the presence of her icy mother-in-law.'

'What are you talking about?' Sam looked at me with concern. 'You live in a delusional world.' She started pacing in front of me impatiently. I was not allowed to read and although we had hours before departure, she wanted to wait at our gate.

To me it was clear, I was not going home! I would stay here in Spain, but how could I organise this? We passed a kiosk, on our way to the gate and suddenly I got an idea. It was a cunning plan and should work if I played it cleverly. Knowing, I would soon be free, I acted the perfect partner, and completely agreed with her quirky, selfish plans. Though, my plan was also selfish. One thing I learned from all this, I now know for sure, was that we didn't fit at all. Sam would be much better off with an easy-going guy, who would be okay to raise my child.

Here, I had to force myself to consider this, but I persevered and then thought it was a good idea. I didn't want a child, and as long as this child hadn't manifested itself in any way, it wasn't difficult to imagine it as a child of some other guy.

Bored, we strolled around. By the time we could almost board, I pulled Sam into the kiosk. 'Let's see if they have a magazine to read on the plane.' I pushed a Vogue into her hands.

'That woman on the cover looks just like you, Squirrel.'

She laughed, apparently, she thought so too because she didn't deny it. I picked up a copy of Historia magazine and with my right foot shoved my backpack behind a newspaper stand. We went to the cashier, I paid for the magazines, while chattering cheerfully. We walked to our gate, where we hung out for at least another half hour. Sam chatted with some English woman, and I flipped through the magazines.

We were called to board. Sam handed me my boarding pass and I felt demonstratively on my back: 'Shit, damn it.'

'What?'

'My backpack is gone.'

'Jacob, no! With everything in it?'

'Yes, my passport. I probably left it in the kiosk. You go ahead, I'll be right back.' With a doubtful look, she joined the queue.

Without looking back, I hurried away. In the kiosk my backpack was where I'd pushed it. I picked it up and squeezed the spot where the box was. I sighed, with relief. No one had noticed. Unobtrusively I walked towards the stream of arriving passengers into the arrival's hall. While they waited to drop off their luggage, I walked out, through the revolving doors.

Somewhere under an awning, I waited in the shade. Even

outside, I heard the metallic airport voice calling my name: I had to go to gate eleven immediately!

'I'm not coming, Squirrel, this time you've lost your power over me,' I childishly grinned against the steel-blue evening sky above my head.

Finally. More than an hour late, Iberia's plane lifted off, direction London. In my mind's eye, I saw Sam sitting, biting her anger, her freckles turned pale with frustration; her eyes might be red from crying, but I didn't really believe that. As the plane veered north and its white tail of water vapor frayed in the air, I breathed a sigh of relief and stepped back into the departure lounge.

BACK IN GRANADA

January 2nd, 1492

That evening no plane left for Granada, a desk officer told me. I felt disappointment, but I could book early the next morning.

Outside the airport, I recognised an Ibis hotel, with its façade divided by rows of black windows. I crashed on the bed and for the first time, since days, I slept undisturbed. The next morning, I opened my eyes at seven o'clock. Nothing but bright, blue sky above the city and I realised, how pleased I was, still being in Spain.

Eager to board, I went back to the airport. During the brief flight to Granada, I experienced Sam's riddance as a physical and mental freedom. Also, rather disturbingly, I feared, if I wouldn't see her for a few weeks, she would shift to the far side of my horizon. I'd even wonder if she'd ever been part of my life. The same was true for my mother, my work, my few friends; in short, I had lost connection with my entire life. And, I couldn't be bothered. Time did that, one became homeless by time travelling. Now, months later, I am free, and not afraid anymore. I now know it was the addiction which pulled me down. My first trips, while using the Sage of the Ghosts, were a major experience, though I had been frightened to be discovered, or to get sick, but it has taught me something. Everything in fact, I've found myself.

Almost back in Al-Andalus in Granada, I was in the cradle of my existence. I knew I was living my last life, but still had some work to do in the past. To do this, I had to go back, and further investigate the effect of the drug, but above all I had to find myself back in that other time. Granada's airport was built on the Vega, west of the city. Santa Fe, the place where Isabella's legions were once stationed, was around the corner. I peered out of the window as if I could already see something of an encampment. As soon as the landing was announced, I closed my eyes and reached into my backpack on my lap, my fingers clasping the box. I broke off a piece of the paste, bigger than I wanted, but knowing it would take a while before the effect would kick in, I took the chunk anyway. I braced myself when the machine's wheels hit the runway and braked vigorously. I wanted to go outside as soon as possible. But there was a delay, someone made a racket at the flight attendant, and the aisle remained blocked. Finally, I descended the stairs, which had been lowered onto the runway. As I stepped down the bottom step, I felt like I was getting off my horse and realised, this was Isabella's army camp, after all. I stood in the dusty sand, blinking against the bright light, joining the throng of soldiers. With their slats in hand, they were waiting outside the kitchen tent. Men in surcoats stood in a long line, some wore helmets, all had swords glittering from their hips. Sliding past them, I disappeared between the white tents, which were neatly lined up. Now and then, a soldier passed me, without saluting me. Indeed, I was invisible. I approached a clearing, a sort of square and a well-known horse caught my eye. Was Boabdil here? The beautiful shining black animal breathed softly, with impatience. I would like to pat his neck and press my fingers against his smooth nose, but I knew better: touching anything would immediately disconnect me from the past.

Two soldiers in chainmail stood opposite of me holding shields. Their helmets were huge. They were standing guard in front of a large and richly ornated gate: the entrance to the royal tent. With long lances in their hands, they barred my way. My polite nod was not answered, and I ducked underneath the lances. My heart was beating fast.

What was Boabdil doing in the lion's den? I shivered in my summer clothes. This was no hot August sun. It must be at least ten degrees colder. In the distance, the sky cut clear and blue along the white powdered ridge of the Sierra Nevada. A wintry sky, which could only mean one thing.

A man in a velvet cape, a leather folder and writing implements under his arm, passed me. He opened the gate, and I slipped after him into the room, which was overwhelmingly beautiful. Isabella and Ferdinand, the royal couple, stood behind a table, opposite Boabdil. I kept silent behind him. The clerk put the folder and writing utensils on the table. Isabella, well over a head shorter than her husband, looked regal just like him. I noticed a slight quiver at the corner of his mouth, but his lively, determined eyes swung alertly from his wife to Boabdil. I could not see Boabdil's face, but his posture had lost every appearance of a proud ruler. With a wave of her hand, Isabella invited him to sit at the ornate wooden table where the secretary had laid out the provisional treaty. Only now did I see Boabdil's eyes, which flew dark and gloomy over the words of the treaty. With a sigh, he dipped a pen in the ink and gracefully drew his name, with the last remnants of his pride left in the final period.

He stood up, defeated. Turning away from the royal couple, he looked at me. His eyes bore into mine, without seeing me. I saw what he thought. He glanced into the future. By staring at me, he visualised what would happen to Granada, to Islam, to the whole world. He saw the blood that would be shed in the centuries to come.

This man had aged many years in a short time. We were almost the same age, but he looked like sixty. Without greeting the Christians, he walked to the gate, I followed hastily, but before he had left the room, Isabella called him back.

'Muhammad, give me the key to the Alhambra.' As if she'd

asked for a book she'd loaned him.

'Tomorrow,' he said. 'Tomorrow.' With the familiar sweeping gesture, he swung the blue cape around his shoulders and yanked the door open. Together we stepped outside.

We blinked at the bright light, shivering for a moment. The emotion that rippled through him shuddered in me too. He mounted his horse, and I jumped behind him. From a walking pace he urged his horse to a full gallop, we raced past the tents. But before we even left the camp, I realised my mistake. I lay on the ground, on my knees, with my head in my hands, facing east, like a Mohammedan. When I looked up, his horse's hoof beat disappeared in a cloud of dust in the distance.

Spanish voices echoed around me. Someone pulled my arm. Dazed, I blinked at the sun and fell back to the ground.

It was over. I was back in the present and totally disillusioned. Still, I had no idea how the sage worked. This time I had taken more than usual, it had started to work faster and had worn off more quickly. Had it to do with my expectations, my metabolism? A full or empty stomach, the time of day?

Two men dragged me off the runway. A gigantic silver bird was towering above me, ready to take off. They delivered me to the emergency room, where a female doctor behind a green face mask, examined me. She looked at me with Sam's gaze. I cringed at the thought of my girlfriend, who was at home and no doubt, pacing furiously around in our living room.

Morayma, the mother

The doctor made me aware of my bloodshot eyes, my pitch-black tongue, and a severe tremor in both hands. She handed me a glass of water, which I gulped down, and instantly nausea surged through my chest. I collapsed back onto the stretcher.

Field hospital, I thought, and sunk into the shadows of the past again. With my arms around Boabdil's waist, I sat behind him on the horse, galloping to Granada. I smelled his sweat and felt his tension slip inside me. Even in the city center he hardly slowed down, which was not without danger; children and chickens jumped aside. When he arrived at the Alhambra, he briefly gave orders. His staff were already packing chests and baskets. Rolled up rugs, vases, crockery, and goblets were standing everywhere.

Boabdil knocked softly on a door, and went inside Morayma's boudoir. He took her in his arms and whispered: 'Our sons can come with us.'

'And Aisha?'

With a hand over his eyes, he shook his head. 'Tomorrow,' he said with a sigh.

'O Muhammad, what will happen to us?'

'It is over. We're going to La Alpujarra, to Laujar de Andarrax. My uncle Al Zagal's country house is ready for us. There, we will stay in exile and wait for the last orders, then we'll prepare for the crossing to Morocco.'

'Morocco?'

'Yes. The kings state otherwise, but I know we will soon

be forbidden to practice our faith and rituals. Soon we will have to adapt to the Christian religion. I don't want that. We are leaving, everybody is leaving.'

'But this is our country, we were born and raised here.' Morayma's face was red and swollen, and her almond-shaped eyes were swimming in tears.

'Indeed. Seven centuries ago, our forefathers settled here, and now we move on. And you know, in less than seven centuries the same will happen again.'

Someone woke me up. A nurse told me, an ambulance would take me to the hospital in Granada. An Andalusian ambulance brother came to fetch me, and I protested. 'It's my own business. I'm fine. I will rent a car.'

'No way, hombre.'

'There is nothing wrong with me,' I tried and pulled myself loose from his firm grip and ran outside. A little further, a row of white Mercedes's were parked along the sidewalk. I quickly moved and said to the driver: 'Granada. Alhambra.'

The cab driver drove me to the city, I sat in the back feeling like a royal, as we meandered up the wooded avenues of the park around the Alhambra. It was like coming home.

I booked a room in the Parador on the grounds of the Alhambra. It cost me over three hundred euros, but who cared. The room was beautiful. For a moment, the shadow of Sam flashed through my mind. She would have thoroughly enjoyed this luxury.

I sat down on the double bed, the box with the sage paste in front of me. I studied the stuff, smelled it, pushed my thumb in the claylike substance. My mouth watered from excitement. Whatever it was, it was too good to be true. I was in contact with the spirit of myself at another time. It was delicious and painful. This was life. It crossed my mind, however, that I was heavily addicted to this Sage of the Ghosts.

I broke off a chunk and chewed. The taste was intense. My heart was beating, my ears were ringing, and I fell backwards on the bed. I wanted to experience the journey back through time. And it worked. My subconsciousness was stronger than my consciousness. Backwards I descended a flight of stairs. Century after century passed me.

Hundred and fifty years ago. I was walking through the Alhambra, a ruin with broken pavement, overgrown spaces between collapsed walls and tattered porches. Crumbling pillars hid under the sprawl of blackberries and coppice. Whole trees grew out of cracked walls.

1850. Washington Irving, sat at a low table overlooking the Lindaraxa garden. Behind him lay the Moorish quarter, the Albaicín. The pedantic American got up and walked, propped up on his cane, through the dilapidated room to the window and stared to the city at his feet. I followed him and was startled by the image. I saw myself standing there. I was Washington, with spiky hair and a golden ring in his ear.

In the gardens I chatted with one of the tenants, a simple craftsman, and tried to determine whether the man was a descendant of a converted Arab, a Jew, or a Christian. His ancestor must have served under Boabdil.

I descended deeper into the past, while Washington Irving slipped further into the future. His most famous and best book, *The Tales of the Alhambra,* still existed with tens of translations in every bookshop of Granada.

Seventeenth century, the French occupied the Alhambra. Numerous cultural changes took place around me. Centuries later, they were praised or reviled, depending on the zeitgeist. I left that time behind and continued walking through the years back to the past.

Sixteenth century, scaffolding stood around the palace of Charles V, the court of the Myrtles was an open space, and a mess. The wall of the arena of Charles V was built just inside the Moorish palace. Only ten days ago, I walked here with Sam along the myrtle hedges around the pond, watching the streaks of light and dark shadows playing tag on the marble floor. The decorative stucco, which resembled bobbin lace, was still beautiful, but the orange trees around the pond gave the patio a completely different atmosphere.

Without knocking, I stepped through a door and entered the sultan's quarters. Under a haze of blue smoke, a group of men sat on pillows. I slipped past them without being seen and entered Morayma's boudoir. She sat in the middle of the room with her legs crossed under her, her colorful silk robe billowing around her. She meditated with eyes closed, palms open on her knees, the black diamond dangling between her breasts.

This was the third time I had seen her. The first time, in Angel's ruin, she had opened her dead eyes. Then, the black diamond had already hypnotized me. What connected me with her? Wasn't she, like me, part of this culture? Was she also born in another world? I circled around her, not wanting to disturb her, just staring at the woman, a mother who cried about her lost children. I'd read somewhere: 'Her eyes were a valley of tears, two lakes that glimmer with sorrow.'

Her eyes were dry now, she didn't see me, but perhaps she felt me, like a breath of wind blowing past; the zeitgeist, an angel in her mind. She mumbled as if she was praying.

'I cry for my mother, who died for her child.
I cry for the rose, wilting in the garden.
I cry for my child, without his mother.
I cry for the night, never seeing the light.

I cry for my love, staring at his lance.
I cry for the power, and the dull shine of the steel.
I cry for my country, that once was, but lost its dreams.
My God, Allah, how I cry the tears from the rain, cold like melting snow.

I cry for my life, not given to me. In my heart full of love.
I cry for death, hiding in the night.

Her sadness overwhelmed me. I wanted to comfort her like a son, who found his mother. I had seen Inez meditating on a mat in her empty, white room. I wondered how much she had loved me when I was a boy. And what my love meant for her?

'You have to break free from her,' Sam once said. 'Your mother is not your wife, I am.'

'I can't leave her to her fate, can I?'

'No. But as her son, you are not responsible for her happiness or misfortune.' I thought that was mean and cold.

'You're avoiding the real emotion,' Sam said.

Emotion? I didn't avoid it; I had no clue what it was.

'You are sensitive, but you act indifferent, or just

sentimental.'

'What should I do? Will I ever get it right in your eyes?' I asked desperately.

Her attitude seemed so much easier, more natural, she knew everything always better, and I was the jerk. She gave me that feeling, and it made me insecure.

Suddenly Morayma left her Buddhist position, and stood up, decisively. She must have heard him, for Boabdil, in full uniform, stood behind me in the doorway. Morayma walked up to him, and he took her hand. He said: 'They're here.'

Goosebumps grew over my skin, tears welled up in my eyes. I was so glad to see him again.

Together they strode to the Mexuar, I followed as their son. Numerous followers in white tunics emerged from the adjoining halls. Outside stood a small army of soberly dressed knights on horseback.

The empty space was a poignant contrast to the past. Where previously carpets and draperies filled the rooms and the afternoon light enhanced the colors, there was now an empty lightness that reigned over the halls. For a brief moment I sensed the poverty of this new consciousness. Where was the Arab sophistication? Had I already entered the culture of which the present was a part?

The handover of The Alhambra

The sun set in a golden sky and in the background, in a streak of light, I recognized Ferdinand and Isabella. The square tower behind them was adorned with royal banners and the Christian cross. The royal couple were dressed in Muslim dresses. Silk lilac cloths enveloped the queen's small figure. Her eyes alertly poked over the edge of the brocade embroidered veil. Ferdinand wore a white tunic, a blue turban, and curled-toed boots. Around his heels hung spurs that tapped on the marble floor with every step he took. Those spurs surprised me. Boabdil never wore spurs. He was master of his mount without this cruel aid.

Morayma, unaccustomed to formal visitors, remained modestly in the background. Her veiled face betrayed no emotion, but I suspected her half-closed eyes were moist.

For me Boabdil was the most interesting. I knew his gestures and actions as if they were my own. Agitated, he threw the cape around his shoulder, his mouth a tense line, and his eyes were radiating a black gloom. He staggered towards the royal couple as if he had been drinking or smoking. The latter, I realised. While Morayma had been meditating, he had been smoking the water pipe in the next room.

The tension between the four royal spouses was tangible. Isabella stepped forward; her eyes eagerly focused on the key to the Alhambra. Ferdinand kept his distance, accustomed as he was to his wife's boldness. Around them stood their dignitaries. In the front row, I even recognized Christopher Columbus.

Isabella spoke first: 'I deeply regret, Oh Muhammad, that we are expelling you from your palace.'

Boabdil carried the heavy, solidly cast key on a satin pillow before him and bowed slightly. I felt his hesitation; should he humbly kiss Queen Isabella's ringed hand? Something inside me screamed: No, don't do that! He didn't.

She grabbed the key from the pillow and said: 'Be aware that every hour of our sojourn, in your palace, we will pay our respects to you and to your forefathers.'

He gave her a weary look.

At that moment his mother, Aisha, who stood next to me, stepped forward. Apparently, thinking the same as I, she wanted to spare her son an even greater humiliation. She cried aloud: 'Your Majesty, save my son your words of regret. He had no choice. Granada is now at the mercy of you and with you our culture will perish.'

'Do not doubt my words, my lady. Thanks to us, your people are safe. If they remain true to our faith and rituals, then we may live together in peace.'

'That is a very unreliable promise!' Aisha said sharply. The two women stood almost nose to nose, each other's equals in many ways.

Boabdil shrugged imperceptibly. As far as he was concerned, this ceremony, this farce, this defeat, was over.

Isabella nodded and made a signal behind her. Two boys, ages seven and nine, were pushed forward. Morayma fell to her knees and hugged her sons. Boabdil put both hands protectively on their heads. As the drums swelled, more than four hundred Muslims emerged, hostages who were handed over to the last sultan.

Disdainfully, the Catholic Monarchs turned away from the Moorish people, and made a dignified procession to the Alcazaba. After they had positioned themselves under the flags and the Christian cross, the Te Deum Laudamus started to play.

I found myself in a dilemma, I wanted to be loyal to my sultan, but I also was curious to find out what the Catholics would now do. The nobles, high lords, the cardinal, and priests, all cried for joy at this gift of God. When I looked back at the sultan and his retinue, I could not think of a greater contrast: the great sadness of the Moors versus the unadulterated joy of the Christians. I suddenly understood, the loss of the Alhambra was equivalent to the loss of a great culture.

'Come,' said Boabdil. 'We'll leave. We have things to do. We must travel to La Alpujarra now.' He took Morayma's hand, and they left the Mexuar with dignity.

A shudder ran down Morayma's spine. 'What about Aisha? Where is my daughter?'

With drooping shoulders, the sultan and his sultana stepped away and disappeared through the court of the Myrtles and the Patio de Los Leones, through the gardens to the exit.

'Yes, where is Aisha?' A woman asked another woman; above their veil, I only saw their depressed eyes.

'Shh, they'll keep her. Special toy for Ferdinand.'

'But she's still a child. The sultana will never survive this.'

I wavered. That moment, that exact moment, felt like the turning point in my life. I now had to choose who to follow. The Catholics? And participate in the construction of their country. Or my sultan. If I abandoned him now, I would abandon myself. He was a part of me. They were my world. I belonged to his retinue as well.

The next moment, I ran after the defeated sultan and his sultana, but they had disappeared into the maze of the garden. I snuck back to the Mexuar. The hall was deserted, I slipped out of the palace and ran to the Alcazaba. Where, on the towers of the Alhambra, the Catholic royal couple stood, surrounded by the invited guests and exuberant revelers.

Al Andaluz was no more. The moon and sickle were brought down, and a great cross was erected. Christianity had won. Aware of this turning point in European history, I watched the scene. It was January 2, 1492. The day Islam was officially banned from Europe.

I made my way through the surging sea of Catholics, pushing aside the Christians dressed up in Arab garb. Near the flagpoles, I angrily yanked the ropes. I couldn't untie the knots and the ropes got tangled. A rope broke. A huge Christian flag blew down like a sail and wrapped itself around me. With flailing arms and legs, I shouted: 'It's not fair, it's wrong, it's stupid. We are all equal!'

But nobody saw me, nobody heard me, I was alone, there was no tower anymore, no view over the city of Granada, and no more Albaicín below me on the right.

The mosque

*I*t slowly dawned on me. I was soaked and tangled in the bed sheets in the king-size bed of the Parador. But I had been present at the handover, the most important moment in Spanish history. My breathing was completely out of control, I panted heavily, my hand lay on my heart, raging like a wild animal. What did I have to do again to regulate it, to come to myself? I started to count. Inhale, count to seven, and slowly exhale again. And again, one two three four five six seven. And let my breath go. The images from my hallucination ebbed away. Suddenly, Sam's head floated before me. Terrifyingly large, like a sphinx on a rock. Her freckles puffed up like pustules, her reddish hair was like twisted rope. Very slowly, her swollen head emptied and returned to normal proportions.

A fever dream, I thought guiltily. Sam. How I had let her down. The carrier of my child. How could I be so heartless. I imagined Morayma's heart opening to her sons, and the shock that shook her body, as she realised she would not get her daughter back. A feeling of compassion filled me. Sentimentally I thought, that's what children do to you, they make you a better person.

I was crazy not to want a child. I had to call Sam right away, explain everything to her. Where was my backpack? As soon as I got up, the familiar wave of dizziness overcame me. The backpack, my only luggage, was on the floor next to the bed. I found my cell phone, turned it on, and crawled back into the tangle of damp sheets. As soon as a network presented itself, I punched her name, the phone rang, I anxiously waited. Sam didn't answer. Her cell phone was off. I called our landline. No answer. Had she actually gotten home okay? I wondered, suddenly concerned. But not for long, I was so exhausted, I fell asleep.

Hours later, I woke up. Shivering. Despite the high temperatures outside, it was chilly in the room. The air conditioning had been blowing all night. I would like to take a hot shower to get warm, but the memory of the contact with water abhorred me. The times I'd washed myself, water felt like chewing gum. Fortunately, the nausea had gone.

I said aloud to the strange figure in the full-length mirror in the bathroom: 'You have to accept that you are becoming someone else. Your appearance is in disrepair, but it doesn't matter.' My inner self was more important and that was fine. Since I was my own company, I was in good contact with myself. 'I'm my own best friend, it's never been a problem.' I peed. I didn't dare to look in the mirror again, and quickly flushed my strong scenting urine.

I dressed and stepped out into the sun on the balcony, and greeted the Alhambra, which was so close.

Groping further behind my facade, I felt how the wall around my senses had been broken. There was no wall anymore that stopped the lava stream of emotions. I could live now with the regrets about my unhappy childhood; in fact, I had even learned a lot from it. Take it as a lesson of life and just forgive everyone. Dad, mom, my half-brothers. Even Sam.

Relieved by this insight, I skipped through the long corridors of the Parador. What a pity, I could not share this feeling with Sam. Was I infected with the euphoria of the Christians?

That felt like a betrayal to Boabdil. I took a cup of coffee in the breakfast room and paid at the reception for the more than valuable night.

Outside, in the morning sun, I called Sam again. Of course, she hadn't picked up before, it had been in the middle of the night. But even now, around ten o'clock in the morning, she didn't answer the phone. Should I text her? But to write what? All the words I came up with sounded banal. Next to me, stood a desperate mother behind a pram with a screaming baby. Last night I saw fatherhood surrounded with tender feelings. But now? Did I still want a child?

I walked down to the city via the Cuesta de los Chinos and crossed the river Darro, up into the Albaicín. Here, I wandered aimlessly through the alleys and across squares, I caught my breath in the shade of a tree and drank water from a fountain at the Plaza San Nicolas, with the splendid view of the Alhambra. I recognized the Alcazaba, where I celebrated the handover with the Christians.

What an absurd situation. Now, I found myself again in that vacuum of timelessness, floating back and forth between my two worlds. I studied the menu of a restaurant where the terrace was filled with tourists. I listened to the guitar plaid by a street musician and then, suddenly my attention was drawn to Arabic singing. I made my way towards the sound and came upon a low, modern, white building framed by fringes of orange flowers and pomegranate trees.

Above me, the muezzin called from the square minaret for the early afternoon prayer. A few Muslims went inside and ritually washed themselves at two octagonal, azure-blue water basins. Curious, I peeked into the prayer hall, lit by candelabra. In the city, I only had seen a few Moroccans. Here, I saw Spanish-looking Muslims entering the mosque.

A Spaniard asked me: 'Curioso?'

I nodded and asked: 'Hablas Ingles?' Do you speak English?

He nodded and shook my hand. 'I am Saíd.'

'Jacob.'

'Fifteen years ago my name was Juan. But now Muslims are back.' He smiled.

I had to let it sink in for a moment because of his heavy accent.

'Isn't it wonderful that this mosque is opposite the Alhambra, a symbol of Muslim power in Spain since 1492.'

'Are there many Muslims in Spain?' I asked.

'More than two million, about twenty thousand in Granada alone. Half of them are immigrants, there are about three thousand Arab students here and we have about five thousand Spaniards who have converted, including me.' His short smile bared yellowish square teeth.

'Do they live around here?'

'No, most of them live in the poor neighborhoods on the outskirts of the city, they go to their mosque there. In 1981 a small group of converted Muslims decided to have their place of worship here, overlooking the Alhambra. The municipality and the Catholic Church created many problems, but finally this mosque opened in July 2003. It is more a tourist attraction. Every week people want to convert to Islam.'

'Really?'

Saíd rattled cheerfully, constantly stroking the black fringe under his chin. I began to suspect that his profession was to persuade tourists to convert.

'Our western world is deteriorating day by day. We are descending into a vulgar consumer society with an inhuman form of technology. Islam offers the only alternative: that of spiritual freedom.'

I nodded.

Saíd suggested something, I had to think about. Conversion? Vulgar consumer society? Yes. But spiritual freedom? I had never looked at Islam that way. Yet, without the political, fundamentalist undercurrent, Islam could indeed be a religion of spiritual freedom. Just as Sufism was the mild, mystical form of Islam, more a philosophy advocating freedom of the mind. Did he mean that? Sufis have no dogmas; they don't want anything to do with fundamentalism and they strive for that one divinity for all religions. The God lives in you. The consciousness of your own soul, which you obtain through meditation, being open and listening to the other. We were still a long way off, I thought dejectedly.

Saíd told me he had to go in. I watched him go inside. Should I wait for him? I wanted to know more about that faith, converting, spiritual freedom. I sat down in the shade and waited, listening to the soft repeating sounds of prayer behind the walls. In trance I drifted into that other world and started to imagine how it would be to be converted.

LA ALPUJARRA

Mondújar

*A*fter the prayer I didn't see Saíd anymore. Slightly disappointed, I wandered through the Moorish quarter, into the city center, and entered a bookstore. The narrow shop was packed with books, from floor to ceiling. The strong smell of printing ink and paper almost intoxicated me. I walked aimlessly along rows of colored spines of thousands of books, pulling out one here and there, that had to do with my past. Reading Spanish was easier than speaking, yet not a word stuck to my blurred mind.

Behind the cash register hung a topographic map of the Sierra Nevada, with Las Alpujarras on the southern slopes. Mesmerized, I stared at that green valley. Twice I was pushed away by customers, who wanted to pay. Then I saw a pencil scribble on the right bottom of the map: 10.50 €. Suddenly, I knew where to go. I had to go back to that valley.

The girl behind the counter took the map off the wall, rolled it up, slipped a rubber band around it, and handed it over to me. I inquired about a car rental company. She told me I could rent a car at the airport.

I called a taxi and drove back to the airport. With some difficulty I tried to remember when I had travelled this route before, as my whole life felt like going back in time.

I left the airport in a blue Ford Fiesta and drove into Santa Fe. A colorless place, where I immediately got lost, and managed to get myself stuck between a container and the wall of some building. Much later, enriched by a large dent in the right door and a chipped mirror, I drove out of the village, onto the ring road. Finally! I stopped swearing when I could follow signs south to Motril.

In the blink of an eye, I was at El ultimo suspiro del Moro. In the parking lot along the highway, I parked in front of Hotel Boabdil, the place I had been with Sam a few days earlier. More precisely, here, on the second day of the year 1492, Boabdil and his retinue turned left into the mountain range on their way to his place of exile. Should I take some sage again? More than last time? My mouth was watering, I didn't have that much left, another trip or three, maybe four. I had to be frugal. What a pity. I would have loved to meet his mother Aisha here uttering the famous words: 'Yes, son, cry like a child for what you could not defend as a man.'

Closing my eyes, to better visualize the scene, I felt I didn't really need the sage. Not here. Aisha stood proudly behind her son, one hand on his shoulder, the other hand she kept over her eyes as she looked north. Boabdil sat like a bag of salt on the rock with his hands over his face. At that moment, I had neither admiration nor pity for him.

It was now clear to me that the sage liberated a lot in me, also the confrontation with the memories of my own youth. Again. It was not Aisha, but my own mother, and the bag of salt was me.

Inez had just been abandoned by my father, who had already moved to the apartment in Nice, to live with Rachel.

'He's abandoned us.' Mother whimpered to herself, pulling the curtains down, rods and all. She threw flowerpots through the room and barefoot, trampling the plants, she sauntered through the potting soil. She opened the China cabinet and deliberately smashed the plates against the wall one by one. I jumped at her to stop her, although I would rather have turned and run away. Dad had abandoned me too. He left me with a crazy mother, crazy as hell. That mother could not comfort me, she was mainly concerned with herself. My father had grown tired of her theatrical dominance and fled into the arms of a trouble-free woman. He could not handle the confrontation. I had to stay with my mother, and he never confronted her.

I scratched my head. From a distance, I looked at myself and remembered a conversation with Sam. She condemned my parents' behavior, which made me defend them again. That's how loyal a child is.

I blinked away the memories of my childhood, and my parents. I didn't want to have anything to do with them anymore. I couldn't live that part of my life again, not even with the Sage of the Ghosts. Yet I knew, deep down, that I had to do something about it. In our quarrelsome conversations, when I was completely unreachable for Sam, she would shout: 'You're bottling everything up. You run away from your feelings, and mine. That big ego of yours. You always know everything better, always the last word, stubborn selfishness, head in the sand, never listening, not really being open, even though you think you are. Go see a psychologist.' Sam's words rang through my head like the ringing of a church bell.

'Nonsense,' I replied invariably. 'Fashion talk. I am my own psychologist. Did you think I don't know exactly who I am?

I don't need anyone.' But suddenly I understood what she meant by that 'big ego' of mine. Everything seemed to be messed up. In my stomach, under my skull, even my legs were like slack ropes. Lost in my own life, my whole ego was like a crumpled wad of paper. I wasn't anybody anymore.

'Don't think like that!' Warned another voice inside me with Boabdil's intonation. 'You are now here in Andalusia. I will show you the way.'

With my hand over my eyes, I stared at the highest peaks. The sky above me was distant and very blue. The light, bright and hard. I couldn't keep my eyes open for long, they stung and burned. Maybe those old sunglasses helped? From my backpack I fished a discarded, scratched pair of glasses and put them on my nose.

Meanwhile, the traffic rushed past me. Could Boabdil actually have seen the Alhambra from this spot? Or had the direction he looked in been important? Had he literally seen the mirage of his past life at this spot? Like I did now?

Back in the car, I drove further south and saw the sign to Mondújar. In this village was the cemetery of the Nasrid family. The little church of Mondújar showed no Arab past at all. Neither did the town itself, which was little more than a sleepy farm village along the highway. I saw a green container for glass, a supermarket with blaring advertising, a bar with a Coca-Cola sign and many other elements that belonged to a modern world.

My guidebook told me that the highway between Granada and Motril had been made wider some twenty years ago, without even considering the legendary Muslim cemetery. I closed the book indignantly. I had wanted to take a lump of sage here, but I didn't dare to anymore. Suppose I ended up on the highway in my hallucinatory state, it would kill me and maybe others. I still had enough sense to realise that.

I started the engine and turned back onto the highway; the next exit was to Lanjarón. Back east, back into the valley. I could breathe freely again.

The past fortnight had been dominated by my quest for the past. Boabdil became my hero, I even dared to call him my alter ego. I had gotten to know him and found him fascinating. Now, I wondered anxiously if I had come to the end of that search, without finding anything. I had taken most of the interesting facts from the various books and brought them to life in my fantasy. Because of the sage, I had lost my girlfriend and ruined my health. Was the euphoria I had experienced during my trips to the past worth it? Had I not risked everything and all for what purpose?

'Every soul is born with a purpose and wants to pursue an ideal,' my mother often said. I had never lived by those words, but now they particularly appealed to me. This became clear to me during this holiday. My aim had been to meet Boabdil, I had put myself in him; and in discovering what had moved him, I discovered what moved me, I thought.

I had reached a new point in my life and had to admit it. I'd made a big mistake. Instead of getting to know myself, I had looked the devil in the eye. The Sage of the Ghosts had seduced and misled me. At this point in my journey, I saw the light, I know now, as I write down this whole story. But then, I saw nothing, just my own misfortune, and still, I didn't want to leave my quest. Allowing myself to change, real change had not sunk in yet.

In the rear-view mirror, I grinned gloomily at the strange sunglasses on that zombie-like head. I stuck out my tongue and was shocked to see how black it was. My hand was shaking on the steering wheel. Every now and then, I felt dizzy and had minor blackouts. Was that because of the Sage, or was it my lack of appetite? I felt worthless. There was nothing left of the exultation, I had woken up with, this morning in the Parador.

The white villages were dreamily lying in a fold of the high mountains. I stopped and walked around, drank water at a fountain. The place was deserted, it was hot, even the sparrows didn't chatter. A few dogs lay listless in the shadow of the church. I missed Sam's energy, her plans, when I sank into apathy, she easily took charge.

I reached into my backpack and searched for my mobile. It was still switched on since yesterday. The battery was dead and the charger was in Sam's travel bag, she had taken home. A telephone booth stood on the other side of the village square. I could call her there. Slowly and with heavy legs, I stumbled towards it. I was at the end of my tether and quite convinced, I had to go home. Home, to the one and only woman in my life, who was probably carrying my child. As I allowed this thought, I cringed at its bitterness. The phone was busy. Thanks God, at least she was home. She was, of course, on the phone with her mother, or one of her friends, discussing my impossible behavior.

For an hour, I automatically dialed my own number every ten minutes. The busy tone kept tugging in my ear. After the eighth attempt, the tone was gone, the phone just rang, but there was no answer.

My disappointment gave way to avenging thoughts. I angrily kicked the bottom of the booth. Glass rattled, so loud, that the two sleeping dogs jumped up, startled, and ran towards me, barking furiously. I wasn't afraid. These Andalusian dogs were sheep in wolf's clothing. They even gave me an idea. Stupid, why hadn't I thought of that before. With renewed energy I strode to the car. I had to go back to where the story had started. Back to Angel and Betty.

The black diamond

Two hours later, I drove into their yard. The turnoff to the path leading to their ruin, I now found, strangely enough, effortless. Halfway down the path, Angel was gathering almonds in a field of almond trees. He watched the strange car closely, then greeted me warmly, as if he'd expected me. Slowly I drove on, he followed the car in my swirling dust. Amid the throng of wagging tails and barking dogs, I got out of the car. We couldn't exchange a word, because of this cheerful greeting, and Angel and I looked foolishly at each other. I took off the sunglasses. He looked at me, as if 1 wore a grisly mask, but said nothing. Then, like old friends, talking busily, we walked to the ruin. I felt happier, glad I could fall back on them in this dreadful state.

Betty appeared, visibly startled, and cried out: 'Jacob, what happened to you?'

'Me? What do you mean?' I said, avoiding her gaze.

'You do not look good. You have dark bags under your

eyes, bald spots in your hair and your clothes are sloppy.'

Looking past her, I said cheerfully: 'I'm fine.'

'Where's Sam?'

'Home. She had to go back a little earlier.'

'Nothing serious happened?'

'No, no.' I answered a bit too fast.

This woman intended to systematically interrogate me. Luckily Angel saved me, he took my arm and guided me to the side of the ruin. He sat down on a large flat stone on the bank of the water basin and pointed to the stone next to him. I also sat down, and like him, pulled a reed from its withered husk. We chewed on the succulent stems in silence. When I thoughtlessly threw a pebble into the water, five frogs splashed into it.

'It's my herbal pasta, isn't it?' Angel asked in a sonorous voice, with a blurry gaze at the water.

I looked at him timidly. 'What is it anyway? And what else do you know about it, besides being hellishly addictive?'

Angel stood up and demanded me to come along. We walked to the other side of the pool, where he pointed to a border of large, fresh green plants, their leaves were slightly wrinkled.

'This is Salvia divinorum. Muhammad and I bought a few plants and propagated them. They grow like weeds. Together we have further developed this hallucinogen by mixing the dried and pulverized sage leaf with poppy seed and argan oil.'

'Poppy? Papaver? Poppy seed? Man, that's pure opium.'

He sucked in his cheeks and stared at the plants. 'Heroin as well. We've experimented with it and applied it to others, always with a buddy watching. What you have done was irresponsible. You should never have used it without someone monitoring. I have warned you. This stuff is no joke.'

'Not without a buddy? I can't remember you saying that.' I shrugged. 'It has brought me a lot, though, this drug of yours set me on the right track.'

'Which track?' He asked in surprise.

I shrugged my shoulders. 'Well, weren't you talking about the truth then?'

Angel looked at me uncomprehendingly. Apparently, the sage had a different purpose for him. I spat the chewed reed between my feet and said: 'I had to meet Boabdil to understand myself better?'

'That herbal pasta shows you what you want to see. Nothing more, nothing less,' Angel said.

'Probably.' I had to interpret my entire experience much more broadly. All those memories of my childhood were a wealth, thanks to the hallucinations. 'I've been through a lot, the paste is almost finished...'

'What?' Angel jumped up. 'Almost empty? Hombre, you took way too much, it will destroy you.'

I shook my head, he was exaggerating, just as much as Sam.

I ignored him and asked about Mohammed. 'Where is he now? Did he use the stuff too? I remember you said he wanted to get in touch with his ancestors. Did he succeed? What did he see? Where is he now?'

Angel looked at me in amazement: 'Yes, he has met his ancestors. Not only here, but also in Granada. He went back to Fez.'

'Oh yeah? Can I visit him there?'

'Well, I don't know.' Angel strode away as if he wanted to get rid of me.

'Does he make a lot of money with it too?' I called after him.

He raised his shoulders. 'No idea. Come, I'll get some wine, and we'll celebrate your return.'

Above my head was the familiar clucking sound of the bee-eaters. Illuminated by the evening light, I saw their colors in a flash: lead blue, ochre, and reddish brown.

I wondered what was going on in Angel. Would he feel guilty for the havoc the sage had wrought on me? I was now very curious about Mohammed; what kind of encounters had he had in the past? Could we share our experiences?

Fez! It shot through my mind again. But of course, in August of the year 1492, Morayma had died quite unexpectedly. Boabdil had taken her to Mondújar and buried her there, then he had crossed from Adra to Morocco with nearly fifteen hundred followers. He had settled in Fez and died there in 1527.

I jumped up. At that point, I came up with a new plan and said: 'Angel, I must look for Muhammad in Fez. I want to know what the Sage of the Ghosts meant to him.'

Maybe we could both meet Boabdil again, there. For the first time in my life, I felt a drive that came from within myself. I wanted something without the need of my mother, or Sam.

Moments later, the three of us sat around a carafe of wine at the table, in front of the ruin.

It was completely dark. Betty smoked her trusty filter cigarettes and talked. Angel rolled a regular joint with weed in it. Surprisingly, the few puffs I took hardly affected me.

As soon as Betty got up and went to bed, Angel reached into his pocket and placed a rock in front of me. I picked it up. It felt heavy in my hand, it was angular and smooth. It glittered black against the light of the oil lamp. I stroked the narrow side that had a hole in it. Then I realised what I was looking at. 'This is the black diamond. Angel, where did you found it?'

He nodded. 'I went looking for it, as you told me. I tore down half the ruin and there it was. This stone was so different from the other stones in the wall. It just had to be the black diamond. Boabdil hid it here, just as you said.'

'So, you believe me, then. It is an important find, Angel.'

'The black diamond comes from Allah and brought happiness to the Nasrids,' he said. 'Thanks to this stone, Granada has remained Islamic so much longer than the rest of Al-Andalus.'

'How do you know that?'

'From Muhammad.'

So that's why Angel had been so bold. At the time he had not given the impression of being deeply interested in Boabdil. However, when I told him how the Spanish farmer had hidden the black stone in the wall, Angel had come up with the legend of the black diamond.

'I think you really went back in time,' Angel said and without looking at me, he filled our glasses again.

In all the books I had devoured thus far, I had never come

across the black diamond. What I knew about the stone, I had heard from Angel.

'Are we rich now?' asked Angel.

'Man, how can you say that. This is the discovery of the century, but I must find Muhammad. He probably knows more about this.'

'Yes, Muhammad was also looking for the black diamond.'

Something started to dawn on me. 'Maybe he used you, to find the black diamond?' And you used me to make money, but I didn't say that. Instead, I asked: 'Do you have his address?'

He nodded and said: 'I'm coming with you.'

'No, you stay with Betty.' The thought of traveling with Angel oppressed me. Luckily, he didn't insist. He even let me keep the stone, which I put safely in my backpack, next to the nearly empty box of paste.

A moment later I sat by myself, Angel had gone inside. For a while, I stared at the stars in that inky blue sky. Above me, a cloud floated loosely in front of the stars, like a white battleship. That ship would take me all the way to Morocco.

Unsteadily, I found the loft where the visitor's bed was, and I fell down on it. Hours later I woke up and looked into the black beady eyes of the gecko. I could tell from the dent in his head that it was the same one I saw a fortnight ago. That night I kissed Sam good night and a little later, I had my first special meeting in the inn. The gecko looked right into my soul. My old soul, the soul of the Moor, who - more than five hundred years ago - stripped his embalmed wife of her shroud. What else did that gecko, with his leathery, stone-colored skin, know?

I pulled my gaze away from that view of the past and tried to think in the 'now' again. Had the gecko shown me the way to the black diamond, then, that night? Was this mythical lizardlike creature the personification of the black diamond? Or from Boabdil?

Over breakfast, Betty insisted I should stay, to rest another day. 'Jacob, you should eat something!' Her maternal concern horrified me. I rejected all their well-intentioned comments and walked briskly to the rental car. Rolling down the window, I said: 'I'll send you a postcard from Fez.'

They waved me off like dear friends, but in the rear-view mirror they quickly faded into my cloud of dust.

Laujar de Andarrax

On the main road, I turned right and drove east, Laujar de Andarrax was my next destination. Here, Boabdil and Morayma had spent their last happy months together with their sons.

Laujar is in the province of Almería, at the foot of the colossal mountain peak, named the Gádor, which is Arabic for 'guard'. As soon as I crossed the border with Almería, and entered this valley, I noticed a different atmosphere. There were mainly vineyards here, no olive trees, and no more almond groves. The villages also seemed less Arab.

In the village of Laujar, I searched for the country house where the Nasrid family had spent their last days. I didn't understand why it was not turned into a tourist attraction.

It was common knowledge that the last sultan was banished here, and his sultana had died in this village.

I walked around the town, through vineyards, which were well maintained, in the French way. I asked a farmer for directions to la casa de Boabdil. He pointed east, I caught the word Victoria and Rey Chico. Yes, Boabdil was also called El Rey Chico, the little king. The farmer had understood me, but what did he mean by Victoria? I went back to my car with some sparks of hope. Heavily pruned plane trees, on either side of the road, guided me out of town. The undersides of their old thick trunks were whitewashed, like Arab soldiers in white surcoats. They waved at me.

I approached the next village and read on a sign: Fuente Victoria. That was what he meant; another village had that name. In the center, a large lilac sign from the Junta de Andalucia drew my attention to El palacio del Rey Chico. My heart skipped a beat. Hastily, I parked in a small square next to a fountain and grabbed my backpack. I crossed the road and ran to the palace. Only a hundred yards further, the small road stopped at the edge of the village. On the left was a shed in which a forge was located. Straight ahead, a dirt path led into the fields, to my right was a Catholic church, unmistakably of a later date, late eighteenth century.

I looked if there were more road signs. Nothing. I turned and looked at the hardboard framed barred windows of a ruin. Here and there, the board had crumbled to eye level, and I peeked in. I could see the remains of slender pillars under a broken bend of what once had been a loggia in an open patio. Weeds grew between broken flagstones. The entrance gate showed spurs of what had been a royal estate but was now half rotten under peeling green paint. I took a few steps back and surveyed the entire property. Not big, but old. Though more than five hundred years? It suddenly seemed a lot of years to me for a poor village like this. I studied a marking tile with a seal over the door, and suspected this must be the palace after all. However, there was no way I could get in. And I even had expected it to be some kind of museum with all kinds of information about the last sultan.

I walked into the fields and fell to my knees due to fatigue and lack of energy. I felt extremely strange. Even without taking the sage, I came in contact with the past. Two large stray dogs watched me from a distance. The voices of the past resonated in my head, I felt the presence of the Nasrids around me, though I was still in the present.

To speed up the process, I sought the help of my Sage of the Ghosts and fumbled clumsily in my backpack for the box, as if I was a blind man. It lay against the black diamond. I took the box in my hand and felt its radiating warmth. With my other hand I plucked bits of the paste as if I was peeling glue off something. Thoughtlessly, I kneaded it into a small ball, which I slipped under my tongue. There was only silence. I sat, cross legged, eyes closed, with the diamond loosely in my hand. Slowly, the sounds of the environment began to dawn on me. Birds chirped noisily, a dog barked, I heard voices, followed by silhouettes.

I was back.

A procession of men and women in long tunics and scarves, wrapped lightly around their heads strode past. They stopped just a few yards from me. Two boys frolicked around the group. The eldest climbed on a boulder that rose purple and dark from the poisonous green grass in front of me. I hadn't noticed that rock before. The biggest kid slid down playfully and bawled. His younger brother also attempted to climb the rock, but nearly fell and screamed. His grandmother, I recognized Aisha, came to help him. She lifted him up by the arm, reprimanding him.

A little further, Boabdil watched the scene with a smile. At his side he kept two beautiful greyhounds on a short leash. Beside him, stood a tall man with his right arm stretched out; a big falcon perched on his gloved hand. With his left hand he stripped the hood off the falcon and the beast flew away, circling high and gracefully around us and landing in a tall tree in the distance. Virtually invisible, yet I could see the bird watching us. The falconer gave the boy, who had still tears in his eyes, a chick.

'Hold it over your head,' he said, and whistled.

The falcon immediately soared, approached us, and stood for a moment high in the sky, looking pointedly down at the people below. Then he dove down, fell into the group, snatched the chick from the child's hand, and flew away again.

People applauded and laughed. The child radiated a mixture of pride and fear. Morayma took her startled son in her arms and smiled happily. Though she looked tired and weak. Boabdil, however, seemed relaxed and sunburnt. He clearly enjoyed the outdoors. It seemed to do him good that the heavy responsibility had been lifted from his shoulders.

After a few more spectacular flights, the falcon was caught, and the company slowly started their retreat. I followed timidly. The family disappeared through a fence in the garden. Behind a fanning palm leaf, I saw the straight candle-shapes of cypress trees. In front of it a weathered red tile roof, just like the Carmens in Granada. This was the place. I felt relieved to see the family's home this way. I walked along the garden wall, looking for the gate through which the family had disappeared. As soon as I caught sight of a colored rectangle, I quickened my stride; that had to be the entrance.

A piercing sound screamed in my ears, I summersaulted through the air, fell, and landed on the tarmac.

The accident

When I became conscious, I found myself lying on the sidewalk by the road. Through my eyelashes I saw a car in front of me with the engine idling. Two men were busily talking to each other, gesturing.

Immediately I closed my eyes again and tried to figure out what had happened. This had occurred to me at the airport in Granada. No police, please. I had to get out of here as soon as possible. I opened my eyes and propped myself up on my elbows. The car was a red Audi. Did it hit me? I remembered nothing, felt nothing. For a moment, I saw a reflection in the glossy paint, but I did not recognize myself. The man from the Audi helped me up. I laughed, swallowed the nausea, and pretended nothing was wrong with me.

I understood from the driver's words, he had not hit me.

He had to brake hard because I ran onto the road without looking. After countless exchanges of apologies and many back-and-forth smiles, we both went our own way. I breathed a sigh of relief.

The fountain in the town square next to my car gurgled softly. I drank greedily, holding my head under the strong stream, but immediately withdrew, when I experienced the water as a slimy sludge. I filled my water bottle and sat down on a bench in the shade. This whole affair had ended with a fizzle. From now on, however, I had to be more careful.

The accident had abruptly pulled me away from the past, but my trip was not over yet. Morayma had died in that house, maybe even a few days after the falconry, she had looked very bad in the bright summer light. It must have been this same August light, because in August she'd died.

How would she have gone? I pictured her in a darkened room under a yellow silk canopy. The light had left her eyes, her last words had died behind a faint smile. Boabdil sat next to her, her hands in his. There was nothing left of the fit man from the falconry.

I had read somewhere that Morayma died of a broken heart. Was that possible? A heart could fail, but is that called broken? She had suffered all her life. Her children had been taken from her, her husband had become the plaything of another faith, her mother-in-law had ruled her life.

Mother Aisha came in with her pointed grim face and glanced knowingly at her daughter in-law.

'It has happened, my son. We will wash and embalm her. Then you must take her to Mondújar.'

Boabdil nodded with his head pulled between his shoulders; he couldn't move, the grief paralyzed him.

'The Nasrid cemetery in Mondújar is the last consecrated and sacred ground in Al-Andalus. Morayma can rest there in peace next to her beloved father and mother,' Aisha said, gently pushing her son aside. The black diamond necklace dangled between his fingers.

Two women came in with bowls steaming of fragrant herbs, I smelled a strange mixture of musk and camphor. The women took care of the dead body and wrapped the corpse in white linen. Boabdil stood helplessly aside, but just before her chest and head were bandaged, he hung the chain around her neck and arranged the diamond between her breasts. As soon as the servants had finished, wrapping her in fragrant cloths, they shoved the body into a grey linen sack. Not long after, Boabdil rode off, dressed as a poor Spanish peasant.

I blinked at the harsh light that shone on me through a crack between two houses. In the shade next to me was a boxwood bush, which gave off the pungent smell of cat pee. The smell of musk in my daydream.

The circle was complete. At the end of that day, I would meet Boabdil with Morayma in Angels ruin. For the past few days, I had experienced the highlights of their lives. I'd been swept up in sentimental romance. I had risked everything. For what?

And what about the diamond? Wasn't the diamond the tangible proof, it all had happened. I reached into my backpack, which hung familiarly over my right shoulder. I felt the box with the sage, but there was no stone. Was it gone?

When was the last time I had the diamond in my hands? Shortly before the falconry company approached me. I had been waiting next to the purple rock for the sage to take effect. They had stood right next to me. Then I got up and followed them back to the house. The diamond must have slipped from my hands when I got up.

In a hurry and alarmed, I ran back to that exact place. The grass, where I had been sitting, should be crushed.

'Look at the treetops where the falcon landed,' I said aloud. But I realised that those trees weren't there now, more than five hundred years later. The rock then? On which the children had clambered; that couldn't have just disappeared. But I couldn't find the boulder either. I had no idea where to start looking. Step by step, with my head at the height of my knees, I searched the grass. Everything looked the same. I walked around in circles. At the center point, in the middle of the labyrinth, lies the diamond, I promised myself.

When I looked up, some village women were watching me. Feeling completely ridiculous, I walked past them, with my head bowed, mumbling an embarrassed: 'Buenas tardes.'

I searched the whole car. Between the seats, the backseat, I even looked under the hood. The diamond was gone. I had just lost the black diamond, the only proof of my trips back in time. Stupid fool, I was. Had I ever owned it? I suddenly thought. Had I fabricated everything. Had it happened in my fantasy that Angel found the diamond?

In my mind, I went back through our whole conversation, the whole story. Gradually, I doubted everything; did it still make sense to go to Fez? Looking for Muhammad, if he existed at all? Without a diamond and with an almost empty box of Sage of the Ghosts? An unbelievable feeling of depression overcame me, crushed me and I saw myself sitting with slumped shoulders.

Yet I got back in the car, what else could I do? I started the engine and drove hesitantly off the square, accelerated, and stayed in second gear. A car drove up behind me and passed me, honking. Back to my senses, I accelerated. The journey had to continue. Further east.

ALMERÍA

Meeting Al Zagal

I had to focus on the road, but also wanted to look at the breath-taking scenery. To the left the mountain range became hilly, to the right agricultural and horticultural terraces clung against the slope. I imagined myself in the Andes or somewhere in Asia.

A shepherd with his flock of sheep crossed the road. I stopped and stared at the spinning buttocks of the animals as they lingered, leaped, and trudged moving into the valley. For a moment my gaze hooked on the dark eyes of the shepherd, still a young man. Would that be something for me to do? Sheep herding? For the next few minutes, I mused about the rest of my life.

As soon as I had left the last foothills of Las Alpujarras, a different, and magical world loomed before me: the desert of southern Europe. According to the travel books, the semi- desert of Europe was in Almería. The village of Tabernas was situated between Murcia and Granada. At a lookout point I parked the car and stared fascinated at the whites and greys and myriads of nuances, veined with olive greens, yellows, and browns, surmounted by the lapis-lazuli blue sky.

I instantly was back in Israel. This landscape reminded me of that time. We lived in Jerusalem and during weekends we made trips outside the city into the bare dry desert, with olive trees and Century plants, blue skies, and the scorching heat. Those were the first years of my life. My parents were still captivated by each other, and I was their radiant center piece.

I smelled the dust and sweet scent of orange blossoms again and heard the stillness of the starry nights.

Why my youth again? Why was I, again thrown back to my youth in Israel? I remembered my first school photo, a boy with a sad face, who didn't want anything. I felt abandoned and scared. Fear dominated my life. The contrast between nice and nasty had confused me so much! Had I had a happy or a lonely childhood? Was I a pathetic kid, or a spoiled brat? I would be embarrassed if I had a child like that. The notion shot into my thoughts: If I had such a child? But I didn't want one... Weren't all parents preoccupied with themselves in the first place? Hadn't Boabdil and

Morayma been struggling with the same problems? How would Sam and I do it?

That was one thought too many.

'Still on the run?' said a small voice inside. 'Not listening to the truth?'

'What truth?' I growled. Tabernas was my truth for today.

The clock in the dashboard told me it was almost five o'clock. After my adventure in Laujar and the drive through the eastern Alpujarras, time had moved on. Once, the Nasrids owned a strategically located fortress in Tabernas, where Al Zagal lived until 1489. Then, the fortress fell into the hands of the Christians. I wanted to see that fortress.

It was visible from a distance, the fortress of Tabernas lay pontifically surrounded by the emptiness of the desert, beyond which the white houses of the town clumped together. I found a shady spot for the car and climbed a long staircase. A gate stood ajar, I slipped in and sat on a wall. I used my book as a fan to give me some coolness. Did I dare to take some more sage? Putting my health at risk again. Twice in one day? Ah, what had I to lose. Hadn't I already lost everything? I suppressed my previous thought of Sam for the umpteenth time.

The Sage of the Ghosts burned in my mouth. For the first time I found the sensation unpleasant, and I felt short of breath. Behind me some children were playing, a dog barked sharply. I sat there and waited, afraid of falling, afraid of what the experience had in store for me this time.

The hand on my shoulder almost gave me a heart attack. I looked up into the angry face of my uncle, my father's brother, Al Zagal. A greater schemer could not have existed. He had helped my father into the saddle, then taunted, betrayed, and abandoned everybody. What kind of family were we?

'By Allah, taman ibn il achch, what are you doing here?' He asked sternly.

I cringed and stammered, 'Amm... I want to talk to you. About the strategy.' He laughed derisively.

'Yes, there is still hope to defeat the Christians. Why don't we fight together against them, instead of fighting each other?'

'You think so?' He said. 'Ferdinand has taken Malaga. More than fifteen thousand men, women and children have been taken hostage and scattered across Spain. They say you helped Ferdinand.'

'Me?' I cried out in astonishment and added defeated. 'They say so much.'

'Highly regarded Muslims have been exiled to other parts of Europe and are reduced to slavery. They must now submit to heavy Christian education programs. Our rituals of faith are no longer tolerated. More than a hundred Moorish soldiers have been given to the Pope, fifty beautiful girls were given to the Queen of Naples, another thirty to the Queen of Portugal. Men and women are employed by dignitaries all over Spain; the higher their rank, the better the workers they get. Malaga, our third largest city in the kingdom of Granada, our main port, has fallen. Christian immigrants are living in the homes of the Arabs and took their possessions. This is all your fault, dear cousin!'

I didn't know anything about it, and it wasn't true. From my childhood I remember how my mother warned me about Zagal's lies. His hand squeezed my shoulder tightly, I bowed my head and felt my weakness, my powerlessness.

'That's a great loss,' I said with difficulty.

'Ferdinand is ready to attack the eastern provinces with his army. Woe with you, if you help him now.' He turned around, and added: 'Ah, what's the point, the battle is lost.'

The pressure on my shoulder was so great, I awoke from my trance. The sharp features on Al Zagal's face turned into a good-natured, red pig's head of a Spanish police officer.

'Cerrado, closed, you can't sit here.' He dragged me through the gate to the stairs. Talking nonstop, holding my arm tight until we got to the car. Relieved, I got in. I wouldn't have been able to walk on my own along those steep steps, let alone find my way back.

I nodded a few times, 'muchas gracias' and 'disculpe me' and gibbered a few more sentences that I had memorized, and now managed to reproduce from *What & How* in Spanish. Which again caused a torrent of words from his mouth, I didn't understand.

Finally, he slammed the door. I rolled up the window, started and drove off. I realised, I couldn't drive at all. I first had to land in the now. I parked again. Shit, I was still somewhere in 1489. I laid my head against the headrest and went through the last part of the conversation with my eyes closed.

'Baza was occupied that year,' I heard Boabdil's familiar voice: ''The city held out for a while, but in the end, they had no choice and opted for an honorable capitulation, which they received, thanks to Isabella's presence. The people of Baza even acted as if they had been victorious. Then the Christians boldly marched towards Almeria. My uncle Al

Zagal cowardly fled to North Africa and Almeria also fell into Christian hands.'

I sighed, blinked my eyes, no, nothing to worry about. I was safe here.

'More than seven centuries we knew great power; wealth, high culture, and civilization, but now all was undercut by our own divisions. We had been swallowed up by the barbaric culture that called itself Christianity: a civilization that would torture and kill us because we would think and believe differently from them. In what way exactly are we different from each other?'

Gradually, I felt myself slip out of Boabdil's mind. I left the sea of sepia and azure, emerald and ochre of the Arabian age and saw the dull colors of this time: brown, green and lead grey. I smelled cooking oil and a smelly garbage container. Contemporary sounds penetrated me, a scooter screeched past. I stood in front of a class with students and gave a lecture about Bin Laden. His tall, thin frame popped into my head. In 1992, exactly five hundred years later, that man had made himself known for the first time. He even had said that Islam would reclaim the territory lost to the Christians.

Muhammad died in 632. Through the Quran, he envisioned that Islam should become widespread. That happened successfully in 710, the Islamic Empire stretched from India to West Africa. Via North Africa, the Arabs led by the Berber prince Tarif, crossed the Mediterranean to the most southern tip of Europe, they landed in what is now called, Tarifa. If Charles Martel had not stopped the Muslims at Tours and Poitiers in 732, Europe might have looked very different.

The city of Almería

The ruins of the Alcazar towered in the distance above the city of Almería. From here, El Zagal had led his army. I'd would have loved to go there, but it was a steep climb and just the thought left me breathless before I even started. To the right, above the sea, the sun spread its red glow; it would be dark in half an hour. That was the best alibi.

I had another blackout during my drive from Tabernas to Almería. I couldn't remember anything. I had driven into town on autopilot and had by accident stopped under a big H. It turned out to be the H for a simple Hostel. The room was austere, but clean. I lay down on the bedspread and fell asleep.

When I woke up again, besides being clammy from the heat, I felt old and worn out, and was even feeling a bit hungry.

I went out into the street and sucked the salty sea air into my lungs. Not refreshing, rather stuffy and filthy from cars' exhaust gases lingering in the high humidity. There were many people on the streets and everywhere bars were open.

Lanterns lined the promenade, their light reflected in the water like glittering silverfish. Near the harbour, I discovered a cash register for the ferry to Nador. A timetable next to it told me the first boat would depart at 10:00 am.

On a terrace I relaxed a bit, with a glass of wine and some tapas. Ever since I was alone, the last three days, I had rushed. I acted as if I was looking for something I'd lost, though I'd never owned it. The black diamond? Such a shame I lost the diamond, it was a token of my time travel and now I had no proof of it at all.

Scantily clad blond girls strolled next to burly men who had indulged too much booze and sausages. No wonder Muslims detested Westerners. So did I. I had never really developed a religious sense, but I understood this bit of Islam quite well.

I had to think, sort things out. Why had my obsession for Boabdil and Morayma grown to such magnitude? Boabdil had crawled into me. My conversation earlier tonight with Al Zagal was living proof of that. We were familiar, we were buddies, my being with him had become common, and now he belonged to me, like my grey rucksack.

In addition, there was that awareness of religion, amazing, how that had entered my life. I suddenly thought of the story a Sufi once told me. 'Once upon a time there was a rose bush. It had been planted with care, its roots grew deep in the ground, which had been carefully prepared. The roots were Abraham. When the rose grew, it had to be pruned properly, otherwise it would become wild and not meet the gardener's wishes. The trunk became straight and strong with the right feeding, handling, and pruning. The tribe was Moses. One day the bud of the most perfect rose that anyone had ever seen appeared. The bud was Jesus. The bud opened and the flower was Muhammed.'

I recognized something in that rosebush analogy. Well, so to speak, because I didn't want to be that arrogant to compare myself to any Messiah. But the sum was easy. After all, my early childhood took place in a more or less Jewish community, then at boarding school I spent six years in a Papal Catholic country, then I turned out to be the son of a

Buddhist monk, who later became a shaman in a Christian country. I lived with a girl who had a Catholic upbringing, and now I had come into contact with Islam. If anyone lived in a religiously tolerant body, it was me. I twisted my mouth into a grimace. It almost hurt. How long ago did I laugh? That confusion again, that knot of threads I couldn't untangle. What was I supposed to do?

Sam. My Catholic girl was back in my head. Like a stubborn wave her name rolled up the empty beach in my mind, the wave slid back into the sea, but her name kept reverberating in the sound box of a large shell, which rubbed in the sand of my brain.

I had to call her and explain everything to her, now! I had to make it right? Saying I was sorry, I'd treated her unfairly and was going crazy. With lead in my legs, I walked to the pay phone, which I had seen earlier. I dialed our number. After hearing a piercing ring in my ear three times, I heard her voice. Pulling the thread tight, I held on to the edge of the glass cubicle and called: 'Sam!'

I heard her swallowing in my ear.

I took off yelling and slapped her around the ears with all my just-invented excuses, threw everything out at once. Exhausted, I fell silent. Whispered her name. Repeated my words of wisdom, of whom I had become. Again, and again.

She had hung up, some time ago.

MOROCCO

Fez

*T*he next morning, I woke up with sore eyes, it was difficult to open them. My hands clasped the sink when I saw an ashen, puffy face under a feverish look in the mirror. Startled, I saw my flaky scalp shine through my hair. Pale, cracked lips, teeth too big for my mouth. I stuck out my tongue, totally black. The grey stubble on my cheeks stung at my fingers. There were stains on my T-shirt of which I could not trace the origin. My shorts were stiff with dirt, and stank. The bare feet in my sandals were sooty black, my toenails needed trimming. I pulled out my passport and looked at my photo, taken three years ago. I compared the photo to the face in the mirror. These were two different men. Dazed, I sat down on the bed. I knew who was watching me. Someone from the past. Someone who had failed. Someone who had disappointed his wife. Someone who was not the son his parents had wanted. A boy who had rejected his father and loathed his mother but couldn't live without her.

It was because of Boabdil. Boabdil got under my skin. Boabdil had already lived his life. He would know the answers to my questions. I had to find him! I grabbed my rucksack and left the room. I left the car keys at the counter. Would I call Sam again? 'Why?' I said to the phone on the wall with a sardonic grin. She had lost her last chance. I now had to deal with the real stuff. I had to find out who I really was, and in what time I was living. Nevertheless, I bought a postcard and wrote to Sam: 'I have gone to Fez, greetings Boabdil.' I crossed it out again and wrote: 'See you soon, Jacob'. I asked the man to post the card.

I went to the ferry and caught the boat to Nador. On board were Moroccan families, businessmen and tourist couples. A mother pulled her child towards her, as it got too close to me. A young couple with backpacks moved to another bench. I sat alone again. After yet another disturbing experience, I retired to the top deck. With my elbows resting on the railing and my fists tucked under my chin, I incessantly stared at the white foaming wake behind the ship. I thought of nothing, knew nothing, and only wanted to be the seagull, screeching, and plunging into the foam in front of me. Sometimes he dived under and came up with a fish in his beak. I closed my burning eyes. The engines were stomping. The wind stroked my skin. And I experienced the greatness of my insignificance.

In Nador, the heat blew around me. I wondered if I could take a bus or a train to Fez. The bus looked rickety.

'Come with me, the bus takes hours.' A taxi driver persuaded me to go with him.

'Fine, let's go,' I said. And then he made me wait for over an hour, until he had filled his very old wreck with six passengers. I crawled in the back and was wedged between the door and a long-legged American girl, who constantly blew her chewing gum past me. I turned to the landscape and stared with teary eyes at the horizon of the desert we swiftly passed.

I felt I belonged here, even more than in Andalusia. I now

knew, I was a reincarnated Moroccan guy, who was on his way home. I used to buy halal meat from an Islamic butcher shop around the corner where I lived. I liked the guy. He always told me how he missed his hometown.

What if I moved here? Would my new life begin here? Was that the purpose of this trip? Had the search for my true self become an accomplished fact? Could I only really find myself in Morocco? This was a completely new angle. In the footsteps of Boabdil. I chuckled at that thought. Boabdil's soul had stayed behind in Andalusia, and more than five hundred years later, I had picked it up on my forays into the past. His soul had settled in me and now I would bring his soul home. Suddenly, I thought this was a very plausible and wonderful idea. It completely matched my feelings of the past few weeks. Satisfied with this newly acquired conception, I closed my eyes and dreamed away in the bouncing taxi.

It was dark when we arrived in Fez. Under an inky, star-speckled sky, we were dropped off somewhere on the edge of town. The others disappeared into the nearby Ibis hotel, but I wanted to get into town and walked to the concentration of lights. In no time, I was surrounded by a bunch of guys, who for a little money wanted to take me anywhere.

'Tomorrow, I'll lead you around,' cried one.

'For a hundred dirhams, eight euros.' Another boy waved a fleece jacket at me and said: 'Only two hundred dirhams.'

'I want a drink.' I managed to say in my high school French. They swarmed around me like flies because my sweat must smell like syrup. I chased them off to the next street corner and flung my arms around with wild gestures. A few stayed behind, but before I knew it, others were attacking me.

Finally, I took the offer of one thin, dark man. He had something vulnerable that touched me. Moreover, he spoke a little English, he said he'd lived in Liverpool. He kept his word and

led me to a simple tearoom. We had a glass of mint tea together. A plate of goat meat was placed in front of me. Starving, I started to eat. With relish - flashed through my mind.

Abdul, that was his name, was thirty-five years old. He told me about his life in Fez. The poverty, hunger, boredom, and division between rich and poor. He was able to describe the hopelessness in a few words so strikingly, I stared at him with my mouth open. I ordered a plate of food for him. We drank more tea. He arranged a room for me, and we said goodnight.

The medina

*T*he next morning, an important thought floated into the unbridled chaos of my mind. Muhammad! I had to look for him. From my rucksack I dug up the piece of paper with Angel's scribbles and put the note into my wallet.

Still sleepy, I stepped into the bright morning light and looked down in surprise at Abdul's curly crown. He sat on the sidewalk, anxiously watching the tattered door of my quarters. As soon as he saw me, he jumped up and shook my hand: 'For fifty dirhams I will take you anywhere.'

I gave him double in euro coins. With a blissful grin he

tucked the money deep into his trouser pocket, although it didn't help him much. Later, I would reward him better, I promised myself.

As if we were best friends, he led me through a large gate into the medina. As soon as the thick walls embraced me, I lost all sense of direction and perspective. The smells of wood fired bread ovens, lamb stews, goat's blood, intoxicated me. Sweating mules trudged beneath loads of tanned hides or modern refrigerators and wherever I looked, something happened. Abdul grabbed my arm and pulled me into a teahouse, as he saw me struggling. He made me drink a glass of green tea with mint and eat some sweet bread. I felt better, my eyes popped back into my head. We were able to continue. My new friend, guided me through alleys and past stalls. I became obsessed by the light streaking through the makeshift bamboo lattice roofs over displays of goat's heads, hooves and entrails, fresh cheese, plenty of fresh fruits, and piles of dried mint leaves.

We walked through an alley with shops packed with colorful clothes. Tailors with their legs crossed underneath them, were sitting here on low tables. In a shop the size of a cupboard, Abdul pointed out a beautiful djellaba to me. I agreed with him, I had to wear one. Without much haggling, I bought the dress, probably too expensive. Too late I understood the man was an acquaintance of Abdul. I pulled the djellaba over my head and instantly felt better, with my shorts and grubby T-shirt hidden underneath.

In yet another alley, shoemakers sat among piles of leather in yellow, red, blue, and brown. I bought a pair of red pointed babouches, covered with gold thread. Abdul said, with a grin, I looked exactly like an old Arab now. He had no idea, the great favour he did to me by saying this. Though, others might have been offended. We actually had real contact, his English became better and I understood him perfectly well.

We penetrated deeper into the medina, meandering past leatherworkers, woodcarvers, weavers, engravers and calligraphers, seamstresses, and an endless line of crafts, I didn't know existed. Professions were grouped per alley. Here and there were merchants with huge scales, offering their services.

The bustle, the noise, the smells of this ancient world, were addictive. I caught a glimpse of the soul of an ancient city. But I wanted to expose the whole soul, as if I was going to undress a beautiful woman. These colors, smells and sounds complemented the images I had had in medieval Granada.

A donkey driver passed, yelling, praising his merchandise. To the flanks of his mule, two bright red buckets were tied, in which glowed something indefinable. I was pressed against a wall, Abdul walked on, and I lost sight of him. Everything twirled before my eyes, staggering I clung to the wall until someone caught me. Abdul. He dashed me to a small square and put me in the shade. Abdul watched me like a lioness guarding her cub.

I knew it was another blackout, but I waved my hand before his concerned eyes, and said with a laugh: 'It's the heat and the hustle and bustle around me.' I puffed theatrically, 'wow, am I thirsty.'

He ran off and came back with a bottle of water. Ten dirhams. I pulled out my wallet and my eye fell at the slip of paper with Muhammad's address. I showed it to Abdul, he studied the handwriting and struggled to decipher the words. Then a wide grin split his face in two. He knew where that was. 'Nearby.' He pulled me to my feet and led me deeper and deeper into the labyrinth of the medina, where the alchemists were sitting. Men behind large bellows kept fires going for coppersmiths, goldsmiths, and silversmiths. On a table stood glass balls and numerous chemical devices, shrouded in yellow sulphur fumes and blue flames. This was my land! Without my hallucinations, I could easily travel back through smells and images only.

Mesmerized, I stopped to watch a stream of blood, rippling between my feet passing the merchandisers, making its way down. Abdul had adjusted to my slow sauntering and said with a laugh at my surprised face: 'This is the paint alley.'

Strands of wool and silk were drying on wooden bars. The warm shades of red, brown, and yellow from the earth, blue from the sky, and green from the leaves, fascinated me. Two men tipped over a barrel and let the wine-red paint run off.

Inez would love it here; I couldn't help thinking.

We stopped at Musta, Abdul's uncle, a rope weaver. The old guy sat on a wooden platform, a metre above the ground with his legs crossed. He tied strands of silk around his big toe. With great patience, he plaited them into prayer cords or loops for caftans.

'He's been doing this since he was ten,' Abdul said. 'Now he's sixty.'

I bought some yarn for Inez. I thought she'd appreciate the gesture, though I had no idea when or where I'd see her again.

In the heart of the medina, stood the largest and oldest

mosque in Morocco, the Karaouine Mosque.

'The wealthy Fatima Alfehri fled Tunisia and founded this place of worship in 859. With its large library, it became the center of study, even before the universities of Bologna and Oxford became famous,' Abdul proudly told me.

'I want to go in,' I said, preparing to push open the huge door.

'Non-Muslims are not allowed in.'

The disappointment stung. The next hour, we circled around the huge building, I tried to peek in through cracks in doors. In patios, I saw trees and fountains, colored tiles and ceramic vases. Somewhere, I surveyed the length of a corridor with niches and domes, streaks of shadow and light. What a beauty. What an ambience.

'It can hold up to 20,000 people,' Abdul said.

Exhausted, I fell in the grass under a tree. 'Abdul, I would like to walk around here for days, but my mind, my eyes, and my ears, even my nose are packed with all the impressions. I can't take it anymore. Please take me to the address?'

We crossed a small square and passed a spice market. As I rubbed my hand against the pumice stones piled up in a stall, Abdul pointed to a large building. 'Once it was a famous psychiatric hospital, the oldest in the world.'

'Nice to know,' I commented, wondering what the information had to do with me.

'It's been closed for fifty years; people used to play music outside under the windows to reassure the patients.'

I looked at the building once more. One of the oldest institutions in the world? I couldn't imagine it. I was drawn back to the towers of kohl, tubs of henna, bottles of rose water and spices making Moroccan cuisine so special. At a pile of cinnamon bark, with that wonderfully intense brown color, I stopped and inhaled the scent of my youth.

'The harem women used to rub this in their skin, before visiting their master for the night,' Abdul said, seeing me smile at the young woman in the booth. I smiled because I smelled Inez. I sat on her lap and stuck my nose into her hair with the smell of cinnamon.

We ascended and descended stairs, entered courtyards, ran through alleys, circled squares, slid past buildings and suddenly we towered above the city. Panting, I put my fingers against my stinging side, trying to regulate my breath, just like I did in the flamenco bar in Granada. Meanwhile, I stared at the silhouette of Fez, before me. The domes and minarets faded into the floating veils of smoke from the ovens and steam from the bathhouses. The hammering of metalworkers, the sonorous beating of looms, the wail of the muezzins calling for prayer.

The old Moroccan

A gulf of feelings descended on me, when I noticed the old man under the orange tree. I was so entangled in impressions; it almost made me mad.

Almost.

I staggered over to him and squatted down so that our faces were level.

'Do you know Muhammad?' I asked in Arabic. I was no

longer surprised whether I invented that language on the spot, or just spoke it.

The man pointed to himself.

'Yes, yes, I know,' I said impatiently. After all, everyone is called Muhammad. He smiled mumbling at me and nodded.

When I got over my first restlessness, I took a good look at him. I knew who it was who sat in front of me. An old man, but unmistakably Boabdil.

'Baba,' I said with a sincerity that hardly surprised me. 'Finally, I found you.'

'Walad, my son. I spend my days in idleness, here under the orange tree, waiting for you. When I inhale the incomparable scent of the azahara, it takes me back to the days when I still lived in Al-Andalus and stayed in the Alhambra.'

'I have missed you.'

'I've failed you. You deserved another childhood.'

I gestured; it didn't matter anymore. 'Baba, I have become, who I am. There's no point looking back and regretting things you wish you had done differently, right? Are you sorry?'

'Ah, yes and no.' He put his hand on my shoulder. I realised he was really talking to me. My father, my spirit.

'Why don't you write your memoirs?' I asked.

'Memoirs? By Allah, son. But that is a lot of work.'

'But with your death, an important part of history will disappear into the grave.'

He sighed. 'You're right. Ferdinand and Isabella destroyed us, burned, and covered our tracks. The Nasrids were once powerful rulers of Granada, rich, loved, and reviled. They were banished, had to flee, or they were killed. They did all three with me. I was spiritually murdered, exiled and then they let me run. Living in the here and now, is perhaps my greatest punishment. Every day, I relive a few minutes of my exciting life. It won't let me go. My past is my present and my present is dead. My future? I see reflected in your eyes.'

I listened to him. The man was undeniably Boabdil. My father. My alter ego, my Arab ancestor.

'Listen, my son, I'm only saying this once. After all the ages I have lived, I've been patiently watching and discovered: there is only one God. One God for all religions, and he lives within myself. And in you, in everyone, you only have to see him.'

I sighed deeply, was this it, was that all?

'There is no beginning and no end. We are nothing but dust in the air, the rays of light on material things: man, animals, plants, even minerals. And that light, that energy is the source, the essence of all life. Then and now.'

I tried to grasp his words, realising I heard something universal. Something that had to do with the basis of our existence. The light in our soul came from one God.

'I am dead but live on in the light that searches for you, my son.'

Did he mean I was back to square one? Was I my father's son, who lived on in me? Was I really back in time? Did my life begin again in the year 1527, and did I have more than four centuries to go before I could find Jacob again?

Epilogue

The day is still pristine, the smells of the city waft by. Above my head on a branch, a bird whistles shrilly, drowning out all the other buzz around me. The deep blue sky hangs over the geometric shapes of Fez in front of me: earth tones and the grey green of a single tree.

On my lap I have the black and green marbled notebook. As soon as I became better, I carefully selected it, along with a beautiful rollerball, of which I have now worn out three. For the past few weeks, I've been writing down my story and just wrote the last sentence.

My health is still bad, but I survived. Sometimes, black spots dance before my eyes, like ghosts from the past. Minor blackouts are accompanied by the familiar waves of nausea. Yet this extreme form of self-exhaustion had been necessary. The destructive effect and my servile submission to the obsession were absurd, of course, but the Sage of the Ghosts did give me great insight. In identifying myself with Boabdil, I looked in a mirror and saw a man who lived over five hundred years ago. I gained insight into humanity and saw how a number of molds have been created, reused again and again in every generation. Modern men come from worn molds, the sharp edges are gone. They have evolved and they should know, we are all basically equal. Then and now, centuries ago and a few centuries from now into the future, we will still be the same people with their fears, need for love and attention, their loneliness and lust for power. We are one person. I think that's an important thought.

In my history studies, I was mainly concerned with the facts and the processes. I didn't do self-reflection; let alone I knew what I was feeling. As soon as I got involved - be it the squatters battling the riot police, my mother's birthday, or a girlfriend who wanted more from me after one night. I hid my feelings behind a game of indifference. I turned away from the stage and watched between the wings; meaning I always and everywhere remained an outsider.

During my admission here in Fez and the psychiatric treatment, I found myself behind the wall I had carefully erected. Suddenly, I swam around in my inner mind, like a decapitated chicken, braving the bubbling and swirling lava flow. A terrifying realisation. But I can do it. I'm still doing it and I'm getting better and better.

'Write down your story,' said the psychiatrist at the hospital in Fez. 'That helps you distance you from yourself.'

'What's the story?' I asked, still lost in the chaos of my disturbed emotions.

When you know, you're on the right track.' He walked away, leaving me to my own devices.

Sam always said, if someone lost track: 'He has lost his way, but sooner or later he will run into himself.' I never understood what she meant by that. But that's exactly what happened to me. I had run into myself, punched a hole in my head in an incredible way and Angel's herbal paste had been the catalyst. Without this experience I would undoubtedly have spent the rest of my life as an aggrieved, disappointed, and misunderstood man, insufferable to myself, but especially to those around me.

What had happened?

I wouldn't be here without Abdul. He picked me up under that orange tree in the court in front of the old house. He led me to this institution: a genuine insane asylum in a building without imagination: bare, dingy walls covered with a network of cracks in grey-white plaster. Here, there were no colored tiles and no colored carpets. The black and white checked floor was scrubbed with disinfectant. The iron beds stood in rows in the hall, just like they used to be at my boarding school.

Once, Abdul came to see me, he had taken care of me with the loyalty of a son to his father. And one day, a woman bent over me, a waft of cinnamon passed my nose. She kissed me, with tears in her eyes. Morayma, I thought for a moment, but it was my mother. Not Sam, but Inez had come. Her unconditional maternal instinct had found me. When I was on the mend, we walked through the medina and talked about the old days, and slowly everything came back.

In retrospect, I would not have liked to have missed the humiliation of my personality during my journey through Andalusia with Sam. I was lost, but so was Sam. We walked on two roads that would never intersect and fought for power without knowing each other's souls.

Sam hasn't forgiven me yet. But we remain connected through our child into eternity. In a few months she will give birth to a daughter, Inez said. Sam chooses to raise it alone, but I understood from Inez, I am welcome to come and meet her, once I'm okay again. We will see.

On the outskirts of Fez, I rented a room, with one window looking over the desert. I wrote in my djellaba and described my journey through Andalusia. The story began with our wandering in Las Alpujarras. The meeting with Angel and Betty. The herbal paste (which I sometimes still long for), my lying behavior towards Sam. I feel ashamed.

But everything has a meaning. I had to walk down this road to get to the beginning of wisdom. And there I am now. The finish is not yet in sight.

Wanting to know everything will be impossible. However, during this journey, the two weeks of timelessness, I have moved into the past and dared to let go of myself. I have stepped out of myself and only now I am able to see myself. What I see is emptiness. Facts are an illusion. It's the truth that matters. That one truth, the all-pervading mind. There is only one truth, and it is inside me.

The seed of that thought was sown on the terrace in Seville with Fred and Isa, or perhaps even earlier in the flamenco bar in Granada: where I saw the man in trance and experienced his dance between body and mind. The seed germinated at the modern mosque in Granada during my conversation with Saíd. When I got out of hospital in Fez, the seedling started to grow, I knew what I wanted. Abdul took me to an imam, who was willing to guide me.

I have felt Allah's approval and his guiding hand. I now visit the Karaouine Mosque every day. Islam is beautiful because of its clarity. I need that structure and regularity of praying five times a day. It is only a short moment, because I do not know any surahs by heart. I focus on the light and my inner self; I empty my mind and try to get in touch with that one thing.

Sam will never understand, but I share the spiritual feeling with Inez. My mother understands. She admits we are fragile souls and also knows, He watches over us, because He created us. That is a valuable feeling.

Religion should not be a political weapon. The thoughts of fundamental Muslims are not my world. I only want to get the best out of faith. That's what Boabdil had in mind, I think, but he was alone. In our world today, faith should play that role too. As something spacious, liberating, spiritual, and certainly, not as a means of power.

But I am also alone.

Last words

My partner and I live since 2000 in Las Alpujarras. The history of this region, with Boabdil and Morayma in particular, always captured my imagination. The white villages on the southern slope of the Sierra Nevada were once built in the North-African way with their flat roofs, hanging organically together. With some imagination the Moorish atmosphere can still be felt in this spectacular region.

Angel and Betty really do exist, though I've changed their names. We met them once in their ruin, and had a hilarious evening. They gave me the idea for this story.

Salvia divinorum is a highly hallucinogenic plant of the caliber of LSD, which can be smoked, eaten, or drunk as tea. The plant grows in southern Spain and is increasingly being tried by young people. The Sage of the Ghosts, Angels herbal paste, is a combination of the dried, pulverised leaf of the salvia with poppy seeds and argan oil, and is born in my fantasy.

Mairena, July 2023,
Marjet Maks

Printed by Amazon Italia Logistica S.r.l.
Torrazza Piemonte (TO), Italy

63699373R00143